A SIMPLE SOLUTION

Lieutenant Lowe was no longer surprised or shocked by the peculiar uses that his engineering skills were put to. There need be no inhibitions related to cost or unorthodoxy in the range of solutions. Efficacy was all that mattered.

"What I've got in mind is gas, sir," he said. "It would have to be very quick-acting or they could be out of the rooms to the rest of the building."

He looked up at Mills for approval.

"Go on," Mills said.

"There is such a gas, sir. It's called Charlie fourteen. Kills in less than a second . . ."

TED ALLBEURY

AVON
PUBLISHERS OF BARD, CAMELOT, DISCUS AND FLARE BOOKS

All the characters and events portrayed in this story are fictitious.

AVON BOOKS
A division of
The Hearst Corporation
105 Madison Avenue
New York, New York 10016

Published by arrangement with the Walker Publishing Company, Inc.
Library of Congress Catalog Card Number: 86-5663
ISBN: 0-380-70444-7

First Avon Books Printing: January 1988

Printed in the U.S.A.

K-R 10 9 8 7 6 5 4 3 2 1

To Grazyna,
my wife,
with all my love

PART ONE

Chapter 1

About ten o'clock in the evening of the first of May 1945 Hamburg radio was broadcasting Bruckner's 7th Symphony when suddenly the solemn music was abruptly cut off. There were a few moments of silence then an ominous roll of military drums, and after the announcement of the Führer's death that afternoon, the appointment of Admiral Dönitz as his successor was proclaimed.

At 10.20 p.m. Dönitz himself had broadcast, and ended his speech by saying, 'God will not forsake us after so much suffering and sacrifice.' But the Nazis had forsaken God long, long ago, and as Dönitz stepped out of the radio building into his car he was probably the only man in Europe who believed what he had said. They hadn't even played the 'Horst Wessel Lied' at the end of his speech.

By the time his big Mercedes was halfway up the road to Flensburg it was raining hard, and his motor-cycle outriders were having difficulty in cutting a way through the hundreds of refugees. There were cars in the ditches, some of them still burning and flickering as the flames fought against the rain.

About halfway between Flensburg and the Baltic was a small farm called Dieter's Gut. It had carried that name since the seventeenth century when it had commanded over a thousand acres. Now, it was ten acres of small-holding and a bare living for the elderly couple who farmed it. They had deserted the farm to seek the protection of relatives over the frontier in Denmark, and today the only occupants were a soldier who had been billeted on them two weeks before, and their young maid, who came from one of the Frisian Islands. To call him a soldier was probably unfair, both to the Wehrmacht and to the young man himself. He was in fact Scharführer der SS Max Lerner, aged 26, and a radio operator with a special unit which had been shuffled off to Schleswig-Holstein a few weeks earlier. The girl was Ursula Oster who had worked on the small-holding for two years. She was seventeen, and had come originally from Norderney. Her hair was dark and long, and her big brown eyes gave her pretty face an air of innocence and frankness. But it was the combination of the pretty face and her big firm breasts that had caused all the trouble. Scharführer Max Lerner had been a pest even when the old people had been there, but since their departure his restless hands had given her no peace. It wasn't that she disliked him, but her mother had always said that those kind of privileges were for the man who gave you a roof over your head and food in your belly. And if God was with you, that man would be your husband.

They had both been sitting at the big wooden table in the kitchen while Dönitz was saying his piece, and when it was over Max Lerner had reached over and switched off the radio. 'That means we're buggered,' he said, and the girl looked frightened. 'Is that what he said, Herr Max?'

'No, Ushi, it isn't what he said, but it's what he meant. They're going to hang on as long as they can to let the army get away from Berlin and the Russians. The British or the Yanks will be here in a matter of days I reckon.'

'Which is best, Herr Max—the British or the Yanks?'

He shrugged. 'They're both better than the bloody Bolsheviks I'll tell you that. I expect the British Navy will want the ports like Hamburg and Bremen, and the Yanks won't give a damn. So I expect we'll get the British.'

She was silent for a moment, then she said. 'What will they do to us, Max?'

He looked across at the pretty face and the big breasts that so tormented him. Generally when he looked at them too openly she folded her arms, but he noticed that this time she didn't. And she hadn't said 'Herr'—but just Max. He grinned. 'Don't worry, kid. I'll look after you. We'll be all right.'

And he had stood up and walked over to the big wooden door. It was badly hung and he had to lift it open. The rain was pouring down, and even in the few seconds that he stood at the door his uniform was soaked. He put his head inside the kitchen and said to the girl, 'I'll be out here for about half an hour. Wait for me.' Then he closed the door.

He walked to the barn and took up a spade and then walked slowly across the big field to a small copse. As he walked he could see a red glow in the sky from the direction of Kiel and there were clusters of searchlights criss-crossing the sky. But everywhere was quiet. At the copse he dug a hole about four feet deep but quite narrow. By the time he had finished it was full of water. He thrust the spade into the ground and then stripped off his uniform, underwear and boots and counted the pieces as he dropped them to the ground at his feet. When he was quite naked he threw every item into the hole, and then, using the spade, shovelled back the soil to cover the hole in the ground. Back at the barn he stood in the pelting rain and held the spade so that it was washed clean.

Ursula Oster had been thinking; or at least thought had leapt rough-hewn into her mind, and she had decided, without going into details, that Admiral Dönitz was giving her good warning about the impending disaster. And this, coupled with the memory of her mother's words, had decided her course of action. Max Lerner was the only one who could look after her. There was another side to the young girl's thoughts rather like the day-dreams of peace-time generals with untried weapons in their armouries. They wished no one any harm but they were given to touching the buttons and mechanisms of their unproved hardware. They knew how they destroyed sandbags but not how they destroyed men. Perhaps they didn't work—

impressive weapons, but not lethal. So perhaps just one tiny war? And Ushi Oster felt like that about the God-given weapons of her body. She knew they looked good but would they really work.

Nevertheless when the door opened, and a lean, stark-naked man stepped inside, she was not prepared. Her hand flew to her mouth, and she was about to scream until she recognized Herr Lerner. He walked over to the black stove and took one of the dry towels and started to dry his hair. He stood in front of her as he towelled his chest and back, and he said breathlessly, 'I've been burying that bloody uniform. From now on you and I are the owners of this dump. OK?'

She nodded. Then she saw he was looking at her body and she could see all too plainly that any doubts she had had about the effectiveness of her charms were unnecessary. He sat down beside her on the big old-fashioned sofa and as his mouth met hers his hands were fondling her breasts. At the same time that Admiral Dönitz was entering his new headquarters in Flensburg, Max Lerner was doing the same to Ushi Oster. Ushi Oster dressed, was pretty exciting. Ushi Oster naked was explosive. The big breasts looked even bigger, and it was clear that Max Lerner was her first man. SS-man Lerner had had tarts in brothels before, but they were just sparklers compared with the Roman candles and rockets of this young girl. She had never learnt any rules so she just did what he wanted. And what was best was that she clearly liked it.

During the next days they had seen convoys of vehicles on the distant road to Flensburg. Although the trucks moved very slowly none of them stopped and the war seemed to have passed them by and left them untouched.

Lerner wore the farmer's old suit but he stayed inside the farmhouse most of the time. They had basic food enough to last several weeks, and it was Lerner's instinct that it was best to attract no attention; at least until the chaos of Flensburg had been sorted out.

It was late one afternoon that they had heard the noise of the motor-cycle. Lerner had sent the girl upstairs and then looked carefully through the lace curtains. It was a solitary soldier in khaki and he was riding his bike across the main field to meet the dirt road that led to the farm. In the courtyard he had switched off the engine and propped up the heavy bike on its biped bracket. Lerner could see now that the rider was a sergeant. As the man took off his crash helmet he wiped the back of his hand across his brow. Then he stamped a few times as if to settle his feet, and he slowly looked around the courtyard. He was a biggish man, and as he stood there he gazed towards the farmhouse, and after spitting loudly he stepped out towards the farmhouse door.

Chapter 2

The sergeant was wearing battle-dress and brown leather riding-boots that came up to his calves. At his left side there was a webbing holster that was empty, because he held the Smith & Wesson .38 in his right hand. He looked slowly and carefully around the kitchen, but his gun pointed all the while at Lerner. He was red-faced and unshaven, and there were glints of red in his beard. On his shoulder was a red flash with, in white, the letters H.L.I. Lerner didn't know what it meant but he knew that this man with the little piggy eyes was tough and had to be humoured.

The bulging eyes moved slowly back to Lerner and the hoarse voice said roughly, 'Wo is' der Fraulein?'

Lerner spoke quickly in good English. 'I'm sorry sergeant. I don't understand.'

The sergeant looked at him and then said, 'Come on Kraut—where's the lassie?'

'What lassie?'

The sergeant grinned. He'd been at this game through the Middle East and half of Europe. 'I mean the lassie with her britches on the washing-line outside.'

Lerner realized then how stupid they'd been, and as he opened his mouth to speak, the sergeant fired a shot. It wasn't meant to hit him, it just thudded into the staircase and sent up a cloud of dust. Piggy-eyes said, 'Tell her to come here wherever she is.'

Lerner hesitated, and said, 'Why do you want her? Can't I help you? Is it food you need or cigarettes?'

The sergeant waved the gun and shouted, 'Get her here now, pig-face—go on.'

Lerner called the girl, and she came down the stairs. The sergeant looked pleased with what he saw and waved her over. She came hesitantly and stood still as he looked at her. And suddenly Lerner knew what he had to do.

'Sergeant, if you leave it to me I can make it much easier for you. It won't be much good if you frighten her. She won't mind if I talk to her first.'

The sergeant half turned. 'She your wife, or what?'

'She's just a girl who works on the farm.'

The sergeant looked him over and he could see the sergeant's crooked teeth as he grinned. 'You been giving it to her, have you?'

'Of course, there's plenty for everyone in times like these. Shall I tell her?'

'OK, Fritz, but don't try anything silly or you'll get this,' and he waved the gun. 'Tell her there's some chocolate for her. I'll get it later on. Maybe we'll have a party tonight eh?'

Lerner spoke to the girl slowly in German. 'Listen carefully, Ushi. This bastard wants you. I've told him you'll do it if I say so. He'll shoot us both if you don't, but he'll have you anyway. Try and smile, look like you're glad to do it because he's going to give you some chocolate. Don't look at me after I stop talking. Look at him, and keep him occupied.'

The sergeant was pulling up her sweater with his left hand and she smiled and pulled it over her head. He put the gun back in the holster and his rough fingers closed over her breasts, and she stood patiently as he enjoyed them. Then his hands were at her skirt and she undid the buttons and the skirt slid to her feet. He pushed her against the table and she watched as he undid his fly. Then he was standing between her legs, and as she lay back unresisting he pulled her legs wide apart and was thrusting at her body. She felt him thrusting in her as his hands used her breasts and then as he moved quicker there was a terrible crashing explosion, and a scream that made her certain that Lerner was dead. But it was the sergeant of the Highland Light Infantry who was dead. Or nearly dead. And a white-faced Lerner was standing over him with the gun pointing at him, as if, despite the bright red blood that pumped from the gaping hole in his chest, he might still put up a fight. But the red face was grey now and after a few moments no more blood pumped from the torn chest. The H.L.I. sergeant was taking the high road back to Sauchiehall Street.

Lerner had wheeled the motor-cycle into the barn and they had spent the rest of the day washing the blood from the sergeant's battle-dress. They had dried it carefully in the bread oven and when Ushi had stitched the hole and Lerner had put it on, the girl could hardly recognize him. He looked like a Tommy. He was a Tommy. She had taken in the blouse and shortened the trousers, and then they'd washed them again and let them dry in the fresh air of the barn.

Two days before, Dönitz had sent the signal to General Jodl, ordering him to sign the unconditional surrender. Now all over Europe, there was an eerie, uncanny silence.

He stood outside the barn and looked across the deserted landscape. All Germany was now a disaster area. He'd seen what had happened in other countries; the demoralizing poverty, and the slow starvation. He guessed that for Germany you could really wipe out the next ten years, because hard work alone would get you nowhere. It was 10 May 1945 and, as at the beginning and end of all wars, the sun shone its consolation on the losers, and its warmth on the victors. As he looked across the meadows he saw that already there were yellow king-cups and marsh violets. They didn't realize that they were German flowers, growing in German soil, and without permission of MilGov. The thought of MilGov sent his mind back to the sergeant.

The grave had gone right down to the big stones and the spoil had been carefully heaped on each side. They had put the sergeant's body in at dusk the same day. It had fallen awkwardly and stiffly, and Max had had to put down the ladder and knock the protesting limbs into shape with a heavy spade. But at last it was done and the surface was levelled. A barrowload of surplus soil was put on the small garden, and then the flagstones in the barn had gone back into place.

Lerner was sitting in the wooden rocking chair and the girl was making some coffee. He had been studying the pages of a small brown covered book. He'd been looking at the buff pages all day long. Finally the girl had said, 'What's that you're reading?'

He looked up. 'It's called an AB64 part two, it's the sergeant's identity book.' He closed it and tapped it idly on his leg. 'Going to be our meal ticket, Ushi.'

The girl smiled. He was a smart fellow.

Each day he had gone out for several hours in his uniform taking the big 500 cc BSA motor-cycle. Every day he had brought back small items of food. But on the third day he had come back with paper bags bulging with food and cigarettes. He was grinning as he spread the various things out on the kitchen table. She was delighted. 'How did you do it, Maxie. You haven't been silly, have you?'

'I joined the British Army today, Ushi. I drew my back pay as well.'

The girl looked astounded, and Lerner was laughing as he sat down. 'I'm the official interpreter attached to the MilGov detachment for Kreis Glücksburg. Just reported in, said I'd been posted through Hamburg. No trouble at all. They're delighted to have someone who speaks German.'

'But don't they want lots of papers and orders and so on?'

'No, they're not like us. They're just glad to have the help. Really. There was no checking. I'm in uniform, I'm English because I speak English, and I've got an AB64 part two so I'm a soldier. Let's have a good meal, I'll open the wine now.'

As he pulled the cork he called to her. 'They've given me a small truck so I sold the bike.'

She came out of the scullery. 'How did you sell it?'

'On the black market. Got a Leica and a Rollei and a gramophone—not bad.'

On the Friday he'd told her he was bringing home one of the MilGov lieutenants the next evening for a meal. She'd made a good potato soup and they had had tinned meat and potatoes.

Lieutenant Mathews was responsible for all stores and services for the many MilGov detachments as far south as the Kiel Canal. Before the war he had been in an insurance office. He'd had three years as an orderly-room sergeant at an artillery site near Glasgow, and then he'd been commissioned and sent out to Flensburg. Max said that he was a man of influence but he was very lonely. He could be a useful man, Max hinted, and Max hoped to set up some deals with him.

Ushi had been introduced as the daughter of the owners of the farm. She hadn't been all that impressed herself. He was about thirty and already rather bald, and she thought that his Army issue, steel-framed glasses made him look like the wolf in 'Little Red Riding Hood'. However, as the evening wore on, it became clear that the lieutenant himself was very impressed with Ushi. She had wondered if Max would mind, but he didn't seem to notice.

The following Monday Max had come home late and he sat up talking to her till long after midnight. It seemed that the lieutenant was very attracted by her. So much so, that in return for sleeping with her once in a while, arrangements could be made with Max for permits for scarce materials that would make all three of them rich. Not in Deutschmarks nor Occupation Marks, but sterling and dollars. The kind of figures bandied about represented nearly a hundred thousand dollars, for Max and the girl, in six or seven months.

Ushi shed a few tears. Not because the lieutenant wanted to sleep with her, nor because of the sheer commerciality of it all, but because her Max didn't seem to mind. It turned out that sleeping with her 'once in a while' really meant about three times a week. But as Max had pointed out, two of those occasions would be afternoons, so it wouldn't really interfere with them.

Chapter 3

The man who stood there was well over six feet, broad-shouldered, and the blond hair that blew across his face in the fresh spring wind did nothing to hide the arrogance of the pale blue eyes. The good tweed jacket, the hand-knitted, polo-necked sweater and the grey flannel trousers all spoke of his Englishness. But he wasn't English. The barbed wire stretched across the road, and the big man was looking across at the Military Police corporal.

It was May 1945, Bad Oeynhausen, headquarters town of 21 Army Group. It was virtually intact and rumour had it that it was one of those choice and lucky towns in Germany, like Frankfurt, which had been singled out by the Americans, or the British, to be preserved, to make their occupation more comfortable. The Town Council which had put it on the map fifty years before had not been looking for the kind of guests that it had now. These were takers, not spenders, and the only Germans allowed through the barbed wire were prisoners or servants.

Corporal Anderson of the Corps of Military Police was a new boy. He had not pushed through the Normandy plains nor up the steep hills of the Ardennes. He'd only been a member of the British Army of the Rhine for two weeks. Nevertheless, he knew his job. He was there to keep importunate Germans out. Whether they wanted extra rations, jobs, their property back, or merely to denounce the neighbours, Corporal Anderson's small German vocabulary was usually enough. But this man wasn't having any. The air of authority was unmistakeable. Corporal Anderson had suffered under its British equivalent, from the depot at Woking, to his embarkation at Harwich. Another thing that put him on edge, was that this man spoke with an Oxford accent, and finally he succumbed to the natural pressure of the stranger on the other side of the barbed wire. The man wanted to see an Intelligence Officer. So what the hell. Let him see one.

Lieutenant Wilson, Intelligence Corps, was nearly 22. He'd been taught how to read ordnance survey maps, ride a motorcycle and deal with all sorts of exciting situations. But Lieutenant Wilson spoke good German, and wasn't designed for excitement, and was now second-in-command of the Document Unit. On the front of his peaked hat was a bronze badge with the superimposed roses of York and Lancaster supported by a wreath of laurels, and a scroll with the words 'Intelligence Corps'. A badge described by the rest of the army as a pansy resting on its laurels. The badge had deceived Corporal Anderson, and it deceived the big German as well.

'I'd like to introduce myself. I'm Colonel Munsel and I think I can be of help to you.'

An imperious hand in a fine leather glove from the Officers' Shop cut him short.

'Were you a member of the SS?'

'Certainly not.'

'Were you a member of the Gestapo?'

'Look here, I haven't come . . .'

'Just answer yes or no.'

'No, I was not a member of the Gestapo.'

Lieutenant Wilson was cold, and he reckoned that he knew who the security boys were interested in, and this man wasn't one of them. He rapped his leather-covered stick on one of the trestles holding the barbed wire.

'Now you just listen to me. This is a security area. You've no business being here, and if you don't leave immediately I shall have you arrested by the police.' 'The German police,' he added, as if there might be some doubt about the status of his authority.

The big German looked at the young officer and the muscles at the side of his face were rigid. Then they relaxed, and as he turned he said, 'You stupid little bastard.' And he pushed up the collar of his sportscoat as he walked away down the road under the plane trees.

Captain David Mills, Intelligence Corps, looked, at first glance, a little younger than his twenty-five years. But that was just physical fitness and an active war. It was his eyes and mouth that provided the rebuttal. His eyes were between pale blue and grey, and they seemed to observe without obvious movement. And this stillness tended to be disconcerting. He was a good interrogator, and like most good observers he didn't constantly seek to display it. His mouth was wide for a man, and the well-shaped lips could have hinted at femininity, had it not been for the ridged muscles that bracketed them into a permanently sceptical straight line. It was not a young man's mouth. It had spent too much time disbelieving in silence, and not enough time kissing. But like the violet striped ribbon of the M.C. on his battle-dress blouse, it was a significant clue to the young man's background.

When he stopped the jeep on the hump-backed bridge his driver had waited patiently. Over on the right was a twenty-acre ploughed field. A mixture of loam and clay. At the bottom of the slope was the edge of a copse which ran alongside the road they were travelling, half a mile or so ahead of them. The tip-off had been from a reliable source and Mills kept his binoculars on the far corner of the field. There was a man with some sheep at the edge of the copse, and a German Shepherd loped up the ditch inside the field. As he watched, the dog suddenly turned, and with its head outstretched, barked furiously, as a big man broke from the corner of the trees, and started walking along the hedge at the bottom of the field.

Mills had seen too many pictures of this man not to recognize him immediately, even at that distance. Despite the binoculars he couldn't see his face clearly, but he knew that this was his man. Mills opened the gate to the meadow, and they drove alongside the hedge, across to the far corner. And that was where they waited for him.

As the man came the last few yards up the slope he was looking at the ground, and when Mills spoke, his head had jerked up with surprise. But with no sign of fear.

'Colonel Munsel?'

'Yes.'

'Colonel Munsel of the Abwehr?'

The man stood still, hands on hips, looking at the younger man. 'You must be Mills—I beg your pardon—Captain Mills.' He hesitated, and then went on. 'It wouldn't be strictly accurate if I said I was an officer of the Abwehr, but I'm the man you want.'

'Well, you'd better get in the jeep and we'll be on our way.'

Munsel made no move towards the vehicle, but said quietly, 'Am I not to be allowed to get my things?'

'Yes, of course. You can get a blanket and a razor.'

Munsel nodded, said 'Thank you', and looked down at the ground, idly moving a few pebbles across the path with one elegant hand-made shoe.

'I did actually go to Bad Oeynhausen to give myself up to the Intelligence people there, but when they found I wasn't in the SS or the Gestapo they weren't interested.'

The arrest of Munsel was one of 21 Army Group's top priorities—he was the Wehrmacht's expert on the Russian Army, had connections with the Abwehr, and had helped in planning Operation Barbarossa—the invasion of Russia. 21 AG wanted him a lot, and they wanted him quickly. The thought of him being turned away was too much. Mills did his best not to smile, but it didn't work. It sounded just like 21 Army Group.

'Why did you try to give yourself up?'

'Because I wanted to ask a favour in return.'

'What was the favour?'

'I wanted to get married before I'm made a prisoner, and I can't get married without registering the application, and then I'd be picked up.' The blue eyes looked at the Englishman's face. 'Would that be possible even now?'

Mills shook his head. 'We've just finished a war, and marriages have to wait.'

But the German didn't give up that easily. 'She's the Count's daughter and it's easy for me to wait, but it's not so easy for her.'

Mills looked at Munsel with all the non-conformist distaste of a typical *New Statesman* reader who had just cast the first vote in his life. A vote for Labour and Clement Attlee.

'Well, Count's daughters are going to have to learn to take their place in the queue.'

Munsel nodded slighty. 'I'm sorry that you're prejudiced against the aristocracy, because I'd still like to ask you if you wouldn't think again.'

'Why the hell should I?'

Munsel put his hands on his hips, and was obviously considering carefully what to say. Then he looked at Mills as he spoke.

'For two reasons, captain. Firstly because if you help me in this matter I will co-operate with you, or 30 Corps, or 21 Army Group—whoever interrogates me. And secondly, she may be a count's daughter, but she's just a girl. And she's pregnant. Our child will be born in the next two or three weeks.'

'What type of information are you willing to discuss with us?'

'You know what my job was?'

'More or less.'

'Well, I'll discuss anything that interests you or anybody else at 21 Army Group.'

'How soon are you prepared to be married?'

'As soon as it can be arranged, but it would take at least a week because I think the Count would insist that it was done by the Bishop, and they don't like one another.'

This was understandable. The Count came from the Silesian borderlands and was a cold, arrogant Prussian;

and the Bishop was a sly, greedy, fat, little man who would have done much better in commerce than the Church.

Mills looked across at Munsel—'If I fix for the Bishop to marry you, would that be what you want?'

He nodded. 'I don't really mind for myself. I'd like to please the Count. He probably isn't your cup of tea but he's a man of principle and I've got a feeling that the times we're going to live in for the next ten years, are going to be difficult for him anyway. I'd really be most grateful if you would allow this.'

Mills was doing 'she loves me, she loves me not' with the petals of a small field-daisy. It came to 'she loves me not', and he pulled the head off just for Auld Lang Syne. As he stood up he said to Munsel, 'Come on, let's see what we can do. We'll go and see the Count.'

The German had put his hand on Mills' shoulder for a moment and somehow he hadn't resented it.

The Schloss was pretty, rather than beautiful, and as they walked across the courtyard, the Count was giving orders to a workman. When he saw Munsel he was going to walk over towards him, but when he saw the English officer and his uniform his mouth went into a hard line, and he stood waiting for them to join him. Mills explained the position to him but the Count's face didn't relax, and he turned to look at Munsel and said, 'Is this what you want, Otto?'

'I think it's very good of Captain Mills to allow us this privilege. I'm sure Helga will be pleased, and I think we should both thank Captain Mills for his co-operation.'

Mills was amused by the little speech, because Munsel was obviously aware that the Count and he already disliked one another. Not for any good reason, just instinctively, which is probably the best reason of all. But the Count had been around for a long time, he didn't second the vote of thanks, just looked at Mills with the alert eagle's eyes as he said, 'Perhaps you'll both come inside.'

The living room was large but there was a big log fire, and before Mills sat down he turned to the Count, 'Freiherr von Leder, I'd better speak to the Bishop if you will show me your telephone.'

He nodded and turned, and Mills followed him to the hall. He asked the operator to get him the Bishop of Hildesheim. His Grace was pretty cautious when he came on the telephone, because it was generally him calling the captain for some favour. It had never been the other way round.

They got through the preliminaries and Mills got straight to the point. 'Bishop, I want you to perform a marriage for a German officer, Colonel Otto Munsel, and Freiherr von Leder's daughter, Helga.'

The Bishop was smooth, but a bit silly with it. 'Am I right in thinking, Herr Hauptmann, that the parties wish to be married themselves?'

'They tell me that's the case, Bishop.'

'Well, I shall be delighted to perform the ceremony and all they have to do is to come down here and sign the appropriate forms and they can be married in less than a month.'

There was nothing Mills disliked more than a weak man trying to use the rules to pretend that he's tough.

'My dear Bishop, it's not only they who want to be married. I want them married, tomorrow, no later than midday, so I leave it to you to make the necessary arrangements.'

This led to a flow of protestations about how impossible this would be on legal grounds, theological grounds, and even propriety itself was dragged in. He didn't often have a chance of arguing with Mills and he was making up for lost time. Mills listened to the flow for a few moments and then interrupted. 'Bishop, I recognized, when you came to see me last week about supporting your application for the release of the man you wanted to reinstate your stained-glass windows, that you are a man of enterprise, and that if you wanted something done you'd get it done. I must just rely on you.'

The Bishop took the ball like the expert catcher he was.

'Leave it to me, Herr Hauptmann. Shall we say at eleven tomorrow morning.'

'My dear Bishop, let's say that.'

Mills went back to the sitting room and the two men had been joined by a girl. She was attractive but not pretty, with the aquiline nose and the weak chin that indicated that she was out of some top-drawer. They were introduced, and she made a pleasant, but cool, little 'thank you' speech. And well she might, because she was very, very pregnant.

The three of them strolled down to the jeep and Mills told his driver to bring the jeep to the Schloss the next day at 1300 hours.

Munsel and his captor slept in the same room at the castle that night, and Captain Mills was best man at the wedding the following morning. The marriage ceremony took place in the Count's private chapel. There was a choir, and an organist, and instead of the Wedding March they had Elgar's 'Nimrod' theme from the Enigma Variations. Otto Munsel was in uniform, wearing a Knight's Cross with swords and oak-leaves; and although the sun shone through the narrow windows, it was a melancholy occasion. After lunch even Munsel himself seemed relieved when they were sitting in the jeep. They drove across the courtyard and down the hill to the main road to Hildesheim. Nobody had waved them goodbye.

Two days later Mills got a small package. When he opened it there was a pair of gold cuff-links, engraved with the Count's coat-of-arms, and a small note which said in German 'With thanks for your kindness and help, from Freiherr von Leder and his daughter, Helga Munsel.'

Chapter 4

Mills' HQ in Hildesheim was a requisitioned block of flats facing the Town Hall and the jeep stopped at the concrete forecourt for Mills and his prisoner to get out.

Munsel was given a large room as his quarters. It was nearly seven o'clock that evening before Mills saw him again. Without formalities he had filled in the basic details of Munsel's career. It wouldn't be fair to say that he interrogated him, because he was only too willing to talk. He was a pleasant change from the hooligans of the Gestapo and the SD.

When the war had started Munsel had been a lieutenant in the Wehrmacht but because of his fluent English he was transferred after six months into the Abwehr, and had worked for some time as a personal assistant to Admiral Canaris, specializing on evaluating information concerning the Russian Army. Then he had been called back to work in the Wehrmacht Nachrichtendienst, attached to Army Group North under General Halder. He'd had a tenuous link back to Stauffenberg's group whilst they were cooking up the 20th of July plot against Hitler.

He had completed his academic education at Balliol, and had not been a member of any Nazi party organization. But he didn't pretend that he hadn't wanted the Germans to win the war. One of his main duties had been to keep Army Group North and the OKW up to date on all activities of the Russian Army down to brigade level.

Mills wasn't sure how far 21 Army Group wanted him

to go, and after dinner he went into his office and called Jim McHugh.

'Jim, I got Colonel Munsel today. Can you let me know what you want me to do with him.'

'Well done, David. I suppose he's playing the name, rank and number game.'

'No, he's talking freely. There won't be any problems about co-operation.'

'Sounds too good to be true. Any idea why?' and Mills told him about the wedding.

McHugh laughed. 'You didn't feel it might be wiser to get our agreement at 21 Army Group?' And Mills told him about Munsel's attempts to give himself up at Bad Oeynhausen.

There were a few moments' silence. 'You mean to say he actually came here, said who he was, and he was sent away?'

'So I gather.'

There was a pause from the other end. 'My God, what a bloody shambles.' And then after a pause, 'Do you think he'll go on talking to you?'

'I'm sure he will.'

'What have you covered so far?' And Mills told him.

'Hold on a minute.'

A couple of minutes later McHugh was back on again. 'We'd like you to keep him down at Hildesheim, David. And we'd like you to get a picture of what happened when the RSHA started breaking up the Abwehr. And we'd like anything you can get on his main sources of information about an operation called 'Operation Thrush'. A lot of it will be the usual nuts and bolts stuff, but from what we've gathered from other sources, Munsel was very accurate and up to date on a whole lot of things that had really tight security. Drop everything else you can, and give us a report about this time every night. If you want any background information from us, let me know.'

It was two evenings later that things started livening up. Mills had reported to McHugh at about nine o'clock, and was well asleep when the sergeant-major roused him at about midnight.

'21 Army Group calling you, sir. I think it's Colonel McHugh.'

'Put the call through to me here,' and Mills nodded at the bedside telephone.

'They said they'd rather you took the call in your office for security reasons.'

He padded bare-footed down a flight of concrete steps to the next floor, switched on his desk light, and picked up the phone.

'Is that you, David?'

'Yes.'

'Look, when you reported to me tonight you mentioned that one of Munsel's sources for top level information was an outfit called the FHO.'

'Yes, that's right.'

'What exacty did he mean by the FHO? Where was it and how did the information come to him?'

'I haven't the foggiest idea. It was just one of many sources he mentioned and I didn't pay particular attention.'

'Are you sure that those were the exact letters he used to describe it?'

'What—you mean F-H-O?'

'Yes. Is that what he actually called it?'

Mills thought for a few moments. 'Yes, I'm sure it was.'

'Exactly that?'

'Yes.'

'That means you were both speaking in English.'

'No, as a matter of fact, it doesn't. At that particular time we were speaking in German.'

There was a pause at the other end and then Jim McHugh spoke very slowly. 'David, don't answer in a hurry but try and remember exactly what he called it and how it came up.'

He didn't need to think about it. 'He had just told me that some German intelligence unit had broken the code used by Abwehr agents in occupied Russia. I asked him where the decoded information came from, and as near as I can remember he said "aus der FHO".'

'Quite sure.'

'Yes.'

'Well we'll contact you tomorrow morning early, so stay put.'

The next morning Mills breakfasted alone, and at about seven-thirty McHugh came on the blower.

'We don't know much about the FHO set-up but we do know that it was very high-class intelligence. We'd like you to find out everything you can about it. You'll need to work pretty fast. Joe Steiner says it's almost certain that the NKVD are pulling out all the stops themselves. Every intelligence service in Europe would like to get their hands on the FHO records and its staff, so keep us in the picture every hour if it seems worth it.'

When Mills went back to his quarters Munsel was having his breakfast. It only needed a jar of Cooper's Oxford Marmalade and he'd have looked more the English gentleman than Mills ever would. He looked like a large version of George Sanders, and after their few days together, Mills was convinced that Munsel was only talking because he chose to. If he'd been interrogating him he reckoned that he wouldn't have got that far. Munsel had survived a series of disasters and he'd need a lot of pressure before he stumbled.

Munsel looked across the table at him. 'Well, what's the verdict?'

'What verdict?'

'I had the feeling you were weighing me up.'

'I was wondering about you—not really weighing you up.'

Most men would have pursued the point out of vanity, but Munsel just leaned back.

'Did you get information from the FHO when you were in the Abwehr?'

Munsel looked surprised. 'God no, the Army High Command wouldn't have let that happen.'

'Why not?'

Munsel looked across at Mills and there was a long pause.

'Don't think me rude, but are you pulling my leg?'

'No—why?'

Munsel stood up, hands in pockets, thinking. Then he turned to face Mills. 'The OKW set up the FHO—sort of private enterprise—in fact its correct title was Foreign Armies East and they were in a permanent state of war with the Abwehr.' He looked at Mills carefully for a few minutes.

'I think you want to talk about the FHO.'

'That might be an idea—I don't really know much about it. Let's go into my office.'

Mills offered him a cigarette when he'd settled down.

'Thanks no, I've never smoked.' He made it seem like too small a vice to be bothered with.

'The Army High Command, the OKW, set up Fremde Heere Ost before the war, and it was responsible for military intelligence covering the Soviet Union. When the war started it was run by Colonel Kinzel. He was getting on—in his mid-fifties anyway—and the whole set-up was rather slow and plodding.

'Then in 1942 General Halder used his influence to appoint a new boy. He was a lieutenant-colonel named Gehlen. A real driver, and he turned that outfit inside out in a week. At the same time it had two powerful rivals. The SD, the Sicherheitsdienst, were an SS outfit under Walter Schellenberg, and they had their own espionage and recce units in Russia. But the real rivals were Admiral Canaris's boys in Abwehr Group III. They were really good. Sabotage, infiltration of agents, radio listening posts and deep interrogation—the lot.

'But in six months Gehlen had left them far behind, and Hitler was using Gehlen for all his Russian intelligence.'

'Where were they based?'

'At Mauerwald near Augenburg, then they moved to Zossen and the last I heard they had had orders to move to Glücksburg.'

'Where's Glücksburg?'

'In Schleswig-Holstein.'

'That's where they ended up?'

'As far as I know—yes.'

'Who were the people who ran it?'

'Well the director was Gehlen and the only others I know were Braun and Schmalschläger. There wasn't much personal contact.'

They had spent the evening drawing down the organizational plan of the FHO, and it was nearly midnight when Mills passed the stuff through to 21 Army Group. They asked him to stand by for half an hour. It was Joe Steiner who came back to him.

'David this FHO stuff fits in with what we already know. Munsel's obviously giving you what he knows. We've reported to London and they are desperate to get hold of the FHO files and records. Is Boyle still with you?'

'Yes.'

'Well, hand over to him, and you've got carte-blanche to get hold of this FHO stuff. But you've got to keep quiet about it or somebody will beat us to it. It's one of the hottest things in Europe right now. Let me or McHugh know what you want in help, or dough, or bodies. That clear?'

He hesitated, 'Can I use Munsel?'

'For Christ's sake, David, he's not on our side, he's a prisoner.'

'He's been entirely co-operative. I haven't forced this stuff out of him, he's just talked.'

There was a long pause. 'Look I'm not going to say yes, or give you any authorization. We want that stuff and quick, it's up to you how you get it. But you carry your own can if you make a hash of it.'

'OK, Joe.'

'Maybe. Best of luck.'

Mills spent an hour in the office clearing up the usual selection of problems. A possible underground movement in Alfeld based on the Hitler Youth, a message from the Bishop complaining about the lights for the evening service, a telephone operator working for MilGov who might be a British deserter who'd joined the SS, and the glad tidings that the Chief of Police had been arrested by Mills' unit for being a Nazi in 1932. Long before you had to be one just to survive. And finally a report from MilGov that some Poles were operating an illicit still in Hameln—and the best of British luck to them.

Munsel and he had a good dinner and he did the decent thing and opened one of the last bottles of Château-Lafite that he had tucked away. When it had all been cleared away he dived in the deep end. 'What did you think, Otto, when Hitler invaded Russia. Was he wise or foolish?'

Munsel looked surprised at the question and swirled his brandy round in his glass and watched it come to rest. Then without looking up he said, 'He'd made clear in *Mein Kampf* that that was what he would do. That's what the Wehrmacht was designed for.'

'That's not an answer, Otto.'

He shrugged, 'They're your allies now, so what do I say?'

'The truth, Otto, and they were your allies till you invaded them.'

He was not amused. 'Time will tell. I think he was right. It's them or us, or it was. Now it's them or you.'

Mills poured him another brandy. 'How far will your cooperation go, Otto?'

He looked at Mills speculatively and finally said, 'With 21 Army Group I'll give them anything that helps them, or the Americans, to hold the Russians. I owe *you* my peace of mind so I'll co-operate with you anyway you want.'

'Active help?'

The eyebrows went up, 'What sort of help do you mean?'

'I want to get my hands on the records of the FHO before the Russians do.'

'They're almost certainly in the British Zone, so what's the problem?'

'We don't really know much about the FHO, and we've no idea where the records are.'

'Neither have I—I assume they're somewhere in Glücksburg.'

'Could be—the point is, will you help me find them?'

'How are you going about it?'

'No idea.'

Munsel laughed. 'Only an Englishman would be that honest—yes, I'll help.'

Chapter 5

Munsel and Mills had sat up till four in the morning and by then Mills had most of the operation planned. And when Munsel went off to bed, Mills moved back into his office and called Joe Steiner at 21 AG, and told him what he wanted. Joe checked back the list with him, then he went to bed.

It was eight o'clock the next morning when his batman shook him awake. There was a mug of tea steaming away on the floor at the side of the bed.

'Tell Lieutenant Boyle I want to see him in my office in fifteen minutes.'

'Right, sir.'

It was nearly twenty minutes before Mills was in his office and Blair Boyle was waiting with his usual cheerful smile.

'Blair, I'll be away for some time on a job, and you're in charge till I get back. Is there anything outstanding that you can't cope with?'

'I don't think so sir, but Sergeant Eckstein's got some chap down in Interrogation. He thinks he's a Russian line-crosser. The chap says he's got something important to tell you and he won't tell anyone else. Eckstein feels you ought to see him. Two other people have interrogated him but they think he's just a nut.'

'Who picked him up?'

'The detachment down at Osterode. He was caught right on the frontier.'

'OK, I'll see him on my way out.'

He stood up. 'Anything else?'

'No, sir, I think that's all.'

He went down to the basement which was laid out as a series of interrogation rooms. The sergeant-major took him along to the furthest room. As he went in, Eckstein moved away from a small, scruffy looking man who was standing by the barred window. He had a shrewd suspicion of what Eckstein had been doing, but he didn't say anything.

'Morning, sergeant. Is this the man you want me to speak to?'

'Yes sir, this is the man. He gives his name as Albrecht Weiss.'

'Right, where's your report on him?'

He sat at the table and read through a routine report which could have covered either a line-crosser or an idiot who hadn't yet realized that the Russian Zone and the British Zone were run by two different outfits.

He looked over at the man. He was small, dark-haired, dressed in a shirt and pullover and a pair of old brown trousers, but his shoes were good. Whatever cover line-crossers took on, their shoes were generally a give-away. They did a lot of walking and the temptation to wear decent shoes was generally too much.

'Well, Herr Weiss, you want to tell me something.'

The man was trembling, but after a few minutes silence, he said, 'Just you. Not the sergeant.'

'Herr Weiss, if you have got anything to tell me, please tell me now. I'm very busy.'

'It's very important, I want to help you.'

Mills didn't say anything and finally the man said, 'I write it down. Just for you, eh?'

Mills waved him to the seat across the table and pushed across a pencil and a report pad. The man could hardly write because he was trembling so violently, and it took him a long time to write down the few words. And when he was finished, he tore off the page, folded it across, and handed it to Mills. In a shaky, illiterate, hand it said, 'Die

Russen sind im Besitz ein Liter schweres Wasser'—'The Russians are in possession of a litre of heavy water.'

Mills stood up and said, 'Thank you, Herr Weiss', and put the note in his pocket. He *was* a nut.

It was nearly ten o'clock before the despatch rider came from 21 Army Group. There was a note from Joe Steiner. It just said, 'These are the things you wanted. I've fixed the rest. Keep us informed. Joe.'

He tested the walkie-talkie. It had a fixed frequency, and a single crystal. It was easy to operate and first time round Security Signals at Bad Salzuflen had responded.

There was a civilian BMW on the unit's transport strength and he got the driver to take them the long trek up to Hamburg. There was very little traffic on the roads, but so much destruction, and so many road diversions, that it was already getting dark when they approached Flensburg.

On the check list that had come from Joe Steiner it said that a farm worker's cottage had been requisitioned for them, and it gave the map reference. When they got there it was ten o'clock. The door of the cottage wasn't locked, and as Mills shone his torch around the main room, it was obvious that the occupants had not long left.

He gave the driver a thousand Occupation Marks and told him to get them some food. It took even that experienced operator an hour, and Mills asked him no questions, because from what he had brought back it looked as though the local black market was operated more by the military than the civilians.

Chapter 6

It was a month after the surrender when they had driven into Flensburg. It had been battered by Allied air-raids, but probably because it was right on the Danish frontier its northern sectors were only half destroyed, and it was there that Mills found the command HQ of the infantry division that controlled the area down to the Kiel Canal. Joe Steiner had suggested that he let them know that he was in the area.

Major-General Stewart was not impressed by Intelligence Corps captains accompanied by German civilians, and he offered no help but no hindrance. And that was all that Mills expected. As they walked back to where the BMW was parked there was the stench of dead bodies from the heaps of rubble, and Munsel was silent and pale. It was only six miles to Glücksburg and the small town seemed almost intact. It had a population of just over a thousand, perched on the edge of Flensburg Fjord where it flooded out to the Baltic.

It took the rest of the day to register on the big map every single building in the district and town of Glücksburg. Including farm buildings and abandoned rural property, there were almost two thousand buildings that would have to be searched.

The Black Watch captain, who commanded an infantry company quartered on a farm near to their billet, had listened silently to his briefing. They were sitting at a trestle table just inside the big doors of the barn, and on the side of the barn there were two torn posters. Mills followed

Munsel's eyes as he read them. The first said, 'In der Einigkeit liegt unser Sieg'—'In unity lies our victory'. And the second must have been very old, for it said quite simply, 'Mehr sehen mit Agfa Film'. Munsel didn't take his eyes off them until Mills had finished briefing the infantry captain.

It was only half a mile to their cottage so they walked. The long shadows of evening lay across the fields, and the breeze from the east carried the kippery smell of the sea. As they walked alongside a low hedge they flushed a brace of partridges, but Munsel was so lost in thought that he hardly seemed to notice the whirring wings and the alarmed squawk.

When they got back to the cottage it was the first real chance that Mills had had to look it over. It had been well cared for, and there was about half an acre of orchard and vegetable garden. There was a white, iron table and chair just outside the door, and he suggested to Munsel that they have a drink.

When he had poured Munsel a whisky he watched him drink it down in one movement of his hand. Mills said nothing, and poured him another. As Munsel's hand clamped round it Mills put his hand over the glass and said, 'What's it all about. What's the matter?'

Munsel's eyes seemed to be focused on something far away in the sky, his mouth was half open, and he was breathing through his mouth. His lips looked dry but he wiped them with the back of his hand. Mills took his hand from the top of the glass and Munsel lifted it slightly and then let it clatter back onto the table. He looked across at Mills, the fair hair blown forward and across his face. He smoothed it back with his left hand and held it there. 'You won't believe it, because I don't believe it myself, but this is the first time I've really understood what the war was all about.' Mills didn't say anything and Munsel went on.

'Right now I just want to go home and be with my wife and wait in the countryside with her until our child is born. But up to now I've been content enough to be a soldier.

All through the war it never entered my mind that I wouldn't see Helga again. And now, it's peacetime, but I have got the feeling that it's never going to be the same again. That I shall not see her again. I feel as if I were dead but didn't know it.' He looked sideways at Mills who, slowly lighting a cigarette, leaned back and said: 'The main reason you feel like that is that it's the end of the war, and they don't really need either of us any more. The corpses in Flensburg this morning probably put you off.'

'Did you notice the two posters when you were briefing the infantry captain?'

'Yes.'

'They must have been there for years, and all over Germany. I've seen them all hundreds of times but today was the first time I'd even bothered to read them. Before, they were just things for civilians, and now they look ridiculous, or pathetic, I don't know which.'

Mills stood up and looked down at him. 'Come on. Put it out of your mind. It's over and done with and we've got things to do.'

It took eight days to check the buildings. They found Gestapo records, extermination records and some useful Party records but there was no sign of anything from the FHO. Those records were going to be too bulky to hide easily, and Mills feared they might have to search the countryside for buried material. Munsel and he had covered the whole of one wall of the big room with large-scale maps, and they checked off the numbered buildings against the infantry captain's search reports. Every building, occupied or unoccupied, had been searched but there was no indication of what they were looking for. Finally he sent his driver to chauffeur the infantry captain over to a meeting. It was early evening when he arrived.

They went over the list and the map, again and again, but there was no clue. Then almost in one breath the captain and Mills started to speak. Mills stopped, and said, 'Carry on captain. What were you going to say?'

'I'd just thought of places we haven't searched.'

He laughed. 'So have I. You mean the boats in the fjord.'

'No, I didn't mean the boats, but they're possibles.'

'What had you got in mind?'

'The buildings occupied by military units—our units I mean.'

'But they're already marked on the maps and numbered.'

'Yes, but we have not checked them ourselves like the other buildings. We've left it to the occupying units to check, and we accepted their reports.'

'Right, we'll do the military buildings with you before we tackle the boats.'

On the third day they were checking the billets of one of the smaller MilGov detachments and Munsel and he were going through the officers' quarters when Munsel pointed through a half-open door. 'Now look at that thing.'

It was a large metal-clad radio receiver. Munsel heaved it round to look at the back panel and there it was, a metal plate riveted to the cover which said 'Receiver type 109A Special. Made by Siemens GMBH'.

Munsel tapped it. 'That's an FHO receiver all right.'

Mills went back to the door and read the name outside. The room was occupied by a Lieutenant Mathews.

Mills waved Mathews to sit on his bed and Munsel and he sat on the Army issue chairs.

'Name.'

'Mathews—James Henry—Lieutenant.'

'Army number.'

'7024106.'

Mills leaned back and looked at him. 'Where did you get that radio?' And he pointed to the big receiver. The lieutenant looked across and shrugged.

'I traded cigarettes for it.'

'You know that's an offence?'

'Oh for Chrissake come off it, everybody does it.'

'You didn't answer the question.'

'I just told you I traded cigarettes for it.'

'Where did you get it?'

'I didn't get it direct. I got it from a colleague.'

'Who?'

He looked shifty, and then as the wheels ground he looked self-important. 'I couldn't reveal a name, captain. That would drag a friend in too.'

'Drag him into what?'

He shrugged. 'This. This inquiry or whatever it is.'

'That's surely your colleague's business. Not yours.'

'Well I'm not going to drop him in it too.'

'Drop him in what?'

'This business. Trading with the Germans or whatever.'

'How do you know he was trading with the Germans.'

Mathews was enjoying the sparring about and he leaned back against the wall. Mills stood up and looked at him. There was only one way to deal with smart boys.

'Right, get your small kit and we'll go.'

He looked shaken. 'Go? Where?'

'To Kiel. You're under arrest.'

'For buying a bloody radio set. For God's sake what is this?'

'No, for refusing to assist an investigating officer in the course of an inquiry. I'd guess there'll be six or seven other charges connected with the radio.'

Mathews took off his glasses, and there were beads of sweat across his forehead. It was then Mills realized that there was something to this that he hadn't yet grasped.

He told the commander of the MilGov detachment that he was arresting Mathews on suspicion of trading with the Germans, but all his instincts told him that it was something bigger than that. He phoned the local Field Security Unit and they accommodated Mathews in their HQ building. It didn't seem 'on' for Munsel to be there when he interrogated Mathews, so it was just him and Mathews across the trestle table. Mathews was pretty subdued now, as Mills went through the preliminaries on the arrest sheet. Then Mills pushed the paper on one side and started on the real stuff.

It took nearly an hour to break him down but by then Mills knew it was an Army Sergeant who had sold him the radio, and he'd also discovered that the sergeant had a civilian billet on a farm in the Glücksburg area. The billet was now a designated MilGov requisitioned building and it had not been inspected by the infantry unit. Even at the end of all this Mathews was still looking defensive, as if he were still hiding something. The sergeant would be easier, it seemed that his name was Maclean, and after Mills had taken Munsel back to the cottage he checked the sergeant's billet on the map. It was only a mile away so he walked over alone.

There was a small army pick-up in the courtyard of the farm. The tail-flap was down and the canvas cover was rolled up and lodged in its leather straps. The massive farm door was ajar, and he went inside.

A sergeant and a very pretty girl were sitting at the rough farmhouse table, eating. There was an opened bottle of schnapps, and the glasses were full. The girl saw him first and she whispered something to the man, who looked up at her, and then, following her eyes he swivelled in his chair and looked at Mills. He slowly put his knife and fork on his plate.

'Sergeant Maclean?'

'Yes, sir, that's me. What can I do for you.'

'I'd like to see your AB sixty-four part two.'

The sergeant stood up and fished with one hand in his battle-dress inside pocket. Then he handed Mills the brown-covered AB64 and stood watching as Mills turned slowly through the buff pages. The date of birth made him thirty, and he looked several years younger than that. And one of his canvas gaiters was fastened the wrong way round. The straps were inside. There was something very wrong somewhere and Mills had a good idea what it was.

'Sergeant?'

'Sir.'

He'd got the military bit OK but it didn't suit him. Could be the bad effect of MilGov of course. And then he put it to the test. He handed back the AB64, and he could see the man's relief.

'Do you sell milk here at the farm?'

'Milk, sir? We're not allowed to sell any food to military personnel, sir.'

And it had stood out a mile when he had said 'milk'. There's no disguising the German 'l'. The tongue is spread wide and flat and half of it touches the palate, not just the tip.

'Sit down, sergeant.' He did, and Mills sat in the chair next to him.

'Tell the girl to go, sergeant.'

He smiled a superior smile. 'It's all right, sir. She doesn't speak a word of English.'

'Tell her to go, sergeant.'

When the girl had left, Mills leaned his elbows on the table and looked at the man's face. It was a spiv's face, pale and narrow but with big brown eyes, light brown. A bad sign in dogs and men. And like all shifty men he could look you in the eye with a frank and honest gaze. So Mills started the ball rolling.

'You're in pretty bad trouble, aren't you?'

'I don't understand, sir.'

'Where did you get the pay-book?'

'It was issued to me.'

'You come from Glasgow, sergeant?'

'Yes, sir.'

'What's the name of the hotel at the main railway station?'

He hesitated. 'Would that be the Station Hotel, sir?'

Mills shook his head slowly. 'You sold a radio to Lieutenant Mathews.'

The man looked down at the table and moved a plate to one side. Then he looked up at Mills again, with that frank, innocent look, and he sighed with the burden of martyrdom. 'He very much wanted a radio set, sir. There isn't much to do up here.'

He obviously still thought it was just a black-market check. He was uneasy but not scared. He was used to the military bit in action. He brushed back a lock of hair from his forehead. 'If there's something I could get *you,* sir. It's not easy but I could try. I know a man with a Leica if you're interested.'

'What's your real name?'

The man knew then, that it was more than black-market stuff. The pulse in his neck was beating fast and he swallowed before he spoke. 'The radio was a German army radio, it didn't belong to anyone, not any more.' Mills looked across at him as he spoke.

'What's your real name?'

He sighed. 'Lerner. Max Lerner.'

'What was your unit?'

'I was in an intelligence unit.'

'What unit?'

'Fremde Heere Ost.'

'Where did you get the AB sixty-four?'

'A sergeant came here one day. He tried to rape the girl, and I shot him.'

He didn't need to say any more. MilGov had no idea of even elementary security. They wouldn't have checked on him. Just put him on the establishment and been delighted that he spoke German, and got them whatever they wanted on the black market.

'Who is the girl?'

'She worked here as a servant till the owners fled to Denmark.'

'Anyone else live here?'

He shook his head. 'Just the two of us.'

'You realize you will be charged with the murder of a British soldier and a string of other things.'

The pale, pinched face looked at Mills intently for a few seconds, weighing him up. He decided it was worth a try. 'I could show you where all the stuff is. It's worth thousands. Pounds I mean, not Marks.' When Mills didn't answer he went on. 'And there's the girl. She'd let you do anything you wanted.' His eyes crawled over Mills' face trying to work out whether it was money or sex that could fix him.

'How old are you?'

'Twenty-six. Just over.'

'How long had you worked for Foreign Armies East?'

'Three years.'

'What happened to the others?'

He smiled. 'Everyone did a bolt.'

'And you?'

He shrugged. 'I'd got nowhere to go. My mother was killed in a raid on Köln last year. My father left us before the war started. I was billeted here so I just stayed on.'

'You'd better show me the stuff you've got here.'

Upstairs there were three rooms piled high with tinned food, blankets, boots and shoes, and the ever present Drawers, woollen, long. There was coffee enough to make at least £5,000 on the black market. The girl said nothing when they went into the bedroom. On a long table were Leicas, Exactas and several Rolleiflex cameras and a dozen Blaupunkt radios.

Downstairs again, Mills told Lerner to light the oil lamps and then he settled down to interrogate him.

'What were your duties in FHO?'

'Radio intercepts.'

'No decoding?'

'I had had adaptability tests but I wasn't told the results.'

'Where was the HQ here?'

He looked cautious. 'I'm only supposed to give my name, rank and number.'

'You're not a prisoner of war, you're wearing a British Army uniform—that's espionage. You've also murdered a British soldier.'

This quietened him down again. 'We never had time to set up a proper H.Q. here.'

'Where were the records kept?'
'At the Rathaus.'
'Is that where they are now?'
'No, they were moved.'
'Where to?'
Lerner was tapping his fingers nervously on the table. 'What's going to happen to me?'
Mills played the ball back to him. 'I haven't decided.'
'They're at the castle, about two miles away.'
'Where in the castle?'
'I don't know.'

When Mills got back to the cottage he went upstairs to his room and turned on the little transceiver. But 21 Army Group had no information on the castle or its owner.

However, there was a message to say that the count's daughter had had a baby son. No complications.

When he told Munsel his face had lit up, but not for long. Mills took him into the garden and even in the russet evening sun Munsel's face looked pale. And his mind seemed a long way away.

'What is it, Munsel?'

His face was grim. 'There's going to be so much to do to put Germany right and I'll be rotting in a camp.'

'May not be for long.'

'How long?'

Mills told him the truth. 'I've no idea.'

Munsel stood with the breeze ruffling his hair, and then his hand went into his pocket. When it came out there was a medal lying in his palm. It was the Knight's Cross of the Iron Cross with swords and oak leaves. The black and white edges of the ribbon stood out against the centre strip of red. He weighed it in his hand for a moment as he looked at it, and then he turned, and Mills heard it whir as he threw it with all his strength. The wind caught it for a moment and then it fell into one of the furrows in the ploughed field.

Chapter 7

The drive swept wide and curved to the front of the castle. There were stone steps leading up from each side to the big double doors, and there were fine necklaces of dew on the cobwebs that hung from the dark green ivy. The big door opened easily, and as they went inside their footsteps echoed in the tiled hall. It was silent, like a church, and as they walked through to the main hall a bird flew across and settled on the gilded frame of a large oil-painting. The sun shone through the stained-glass windows, and motes of dust drifted in the rays of light. The doors to a dining-hall and a conservatory stood open, and there was the warm summer smell of damp earth and leaves, from an orangery. Orange and peach trees, and a big vine, covered one long wall. Pools of water lay on the brick pathways, and the pools were covered with thick green algae so that they shone with a brilliant, emerald, green. From the overhead steam-pipes water dripped sporadically, and the drops pattered loudly on the wide-spread leaves of tropical plants. There was no need to search the rest of the mansion, for the recently dug earth alongside a clump of rotting lilies was still ridged at both ends, and the surplus soil was heaped against the wall against which a spade was propped. The earth was beyond the throw of the pipes, and was dry and loose; it had been dug some weeks back, already there were the bright green spikes of new grass scattered across the surface.

* * *

But they had dug deep. Almost six feet, and the sides of the hole were lined with wooden slats. There were four black containers of japanned steel, and the lids were not locked. Inside were the reels of micro-film in protective aluminium cans. They had FHO scrawled on them in black paint. There were 104 altogether. It took an hour to load them into the car, and Mills drove slowly back to the cottage. A light truck from 21AG took them to Bad Oeynhausen a couple of hours later, and Mills had received instructions on the radio to send Munsel under escort to the 30 Corps Interrogation Centre at Westertimke. He decided to break the rules.

They were drinking coffee at the kitchen table when he told Munsel.

'Otto, I've had orders to send you on to Westertimke.

The handsome face was pale and drawn, and he didn't look round as Mills spoke. His depression was near the point of no return.

'But before you go I'm going to give you three days back with your wife and son.'

For a moment the enamel mug clattered against Munsel's teeth and then his hand lowered it to the table. When he turned and looked at Mills there were tears rimmed on his eyes.

'I'll want your word of honour that you'll report back to me next Monday morning. Sometime before midday. I shall say I'm still interrogating you. Understand?'

Munsel nodded, and stood up and walked to the small window. As he looked out he spoke without turning.

'Why are you doing this, Captain Mills?'

Mills shuffled some crumbs on the scrubbed table-top because he knew that his answer mattered. He didn't know at the time how much it mattered, but he knew that Munsel was drowning in a black sea of depression. When he looked up, Munsel had half-turned, and was watching his face intently. He kept quite still as Mills spoke.

'You're tired and depressed after five years of war, and because you've lost. You're frustrated because you know you could help, but you're going to be in a POW cage for the years that matter. You know that your wife and your son are going to be without privileges. So will the Count himself. You weren't a Nazi but you went along with the winning. You helped make this shambles and you know it. You're not even going to get the chance to help put it right. Not for a long time anyway. Everything that's bad, you know is deserved. And you're too intelligent to do what most Germans will do, and blame the British or the Americans, or even the Russians.

'All *that*, is what makes you depressed. If you go into the camp as you are now, you'll slowly get worse until there's no more spirit left. Then you'll just go into a dream world and that will be that. I'm hoping that seeing your wife, and your son, will charge your batteries, and then you'll survive. Probably be a bloody nuisance as well.'

Munsel didn't smile.

'There's more to it than that, Captain Mills, isn't there?'

'What?'

'That you do this at all. That you thought of it, and do it, and you trust me to report back to you.'

Mills sighed, stood up, and picked up his kit and the radio.

'Let's get going and we'll be in Hildesheim before it's dark.'

Munsel reported back early on the Monday and left for Westertimke. He had looked well and energetic. All military again, and very much the full colonel. Mills thought that he was probably going to be a right bastard at the camp.

Every year Mills got a Christmas card from Munsel and his family. Three years it was the only one he got. No matter how many times he moved, the card would arrive at the right address. There was never much on it, just Christmas wishes and three scrawled signatures. The fourth year after he'd left the racket there was an extra name. It looked like they'd had a daughter. Name of Jutta.

PART TWO

Chapter 8

There was an envelope fastened to the outer door of his flat. Scrawled on it in a bold but shaky hand was written 'For David Mills Esq. Private'. And in case there could be any doubt, the word 'private' was underlined three times. As his thumbnail worked at the coloured drawing pin that held the envelope, he was aware of the bright shafts of sunlight that made pools of light in the shade of the foyer. It was one of those superb days in May that spread false rumours of the summer to come. Blue skies, black shadows, bright, verdant greens and a tar-melting heat. It was the third in succession, and there was dust in the London streets, and bus-conductors in shirt sleeves.

The pin flew out and he opened the envelope. He had already recognized the writing. The note was from the old lady who lived in the opposite flat. He pulled out the single sheet of notepaper and folded it open. It just said,

> Dear David,
>
> You'd better look at the 'Fairy' Liquid.
>
> Love,
>
> Sylvia Mortimer.

There was no sound in the flat after he had closed the door. He guessed that she would be either unconscious on the bed, or kneeling at the bowl in the toilet. He walked slowly into the kitchen and opened the narrow white cupboard that held the cleaning paraphernalia. His eyes went over the shelves of jars and bottles but he could see no 'Fairy' Liquid. Maybe the old soul was wrong. But there was a bright yellow duster carelessly or carefully placed on the middle shelf. He moved it aside, and there it was. The slim white plastic pack with the green print. He reached in and pulled it out, scattering small jars and packets as it came. There was none of the normal green stuff caked around the little red plastic stopper. He prised it up and held it to his nose. It was whisky all right, and his guess was Jamieson's Ten Year Old.

He stood there for a few moments and then walked slowly to the white chipped sink. The stopper came off with the help of a spoon and the brown sparkling liquid poured slowly away. If you've ever lived with an alcoholic you don't make jokes about drunks. Not at the time, nor ever afterwards. As the whisky drained away he looked through the net curtains at the ladies in the gardens. They were busy at their talk with many a furtive glance towards his window. It had probably been quite an afternoon that milady had put on for their benefit.

He threw the empty plastic container into the pedal-bin and walked down the hall to the main bedroom. His feet crunched on gravel and soil and he saw that there were flower pots lying broken and empty, their jagged shards mixed with the soil on the hallway tiles. Their gloxinias and geraniums lay with bare, dry, roots.

There was nobody in any of the rooms, but in the sitting-room the water-garden was smashed, and the fish lay stiff and cold on the wet carpet. A copy of Zelda Fitzgerald's *Save Me the Waltz* was open face-downwards on the coffee table, and the turntable on the hi-fi was still revolving with the stylus clicking on the scroll of a record. He switched it off and noticed the title. It was 'Songs for Swinging Lovers'. As he stood up the door bell rang.

There were two men there. One in a tweed jacket with leather elbow patches, brown slacks and a white shirt. The other, who was thinner and taller, wore a lightweight suit, pale grey, and there was some sort of regimental crest in the motif on his dark blue tie.

'Mr Mills. David Mills?'

'Yes.'

'Could we come in for a moment. We're police officers. I'm Inspector Evans.' The brown eyes looked alert but friendly. And he nodded as Mills opened the door wide for them. When the two men were seated, Mills pulled up a chair and sat down opposite the inspector.

'Mr Mills, I think you know Miss Seymour. Miss Jane Seymour?'

'Yes, of course. She lives here.'

'Where is she at the moment.'

'She's out somewhere.'

'Where?'

'I don't know exacty. I expect her back for dinner.'

The Inspector leaned back in his chair and cast a glance at the dead fish on the carpet.

'When did you see Miss Seymour last?'

'Oh, about nine, or just after nine, this morning, when I went to my office.'

'Which is where Mr Mills?'

'In Sloane Street. Just near Sloane Square.'

'Have you contacted her during the day?' It was the younger man who spoke, and the raw, red face looked slightly aggressive.

'Look. I'd like to know what's going on. Why are you here?'

'I'm surprised you didn't ask before Mr Mills. Why do you think we're here?' This was Evans again.

'I don't know. Has she been taken ill or something?'

The Inspector waved a hand at the dead fish and the wet carpet.

'What's been happening, Mr Mills?'

Mills hesitated long enough for the Inspector to lean forward and say, 'Do you mind if we have a look around.' When Mills didn't answer he stood up, and Mills could hear him crunching through the mess in the hall as he went into all the rooms. When he came back he was holding the note in his hand. He gave it to the younger man and sat down.

'Mr Mills, I have to tell you that Miss Seymour is dead.'

Mills' mouth closed in a grim line, and he looked at the Inspector for a few moments before he said quietly, 'Tell me what happened.'

'She drove her car over the causeway and into the river. She and her passenger were both drowned.'

'Where was this?'

'On the south bank of the Thames at Putney Bridge.'

'Who was the passenger?'

'A man named Liam Macbride.'

Mills could see again the weak flabby mouth and the washed-out blue eyes, and he remembered a phrase that Macbride had used which had stuck, grating, in his mind from one of his visits. Jane had left the room and was vomiting loudly in the bathroom, Macbride had sat back, drink in hand, and as the fishy eyes looked at Mills, he had said, 'Jane's such a funsy girl you know.'

The Inspector was looking intently at Mills when he spoke.

'You know Macbride?'

'Yes.'

'Was he a close friend of Miss Seymour?'

'He saw her from time to time. They were friends from back in Ireland.'

'We haven't had a full path. report but it looks like they had been drinking heavily. Is that likely?'

Mills looked across at the policeman.

'Do I have to answer that?'

'No, sir. And this is only to help us to establish a reason. The evidence from witnesses looks as if it was deliberate. Suicide. The coroner will want to know if there were any reasons for her doing this.'

Mills leaned back in his chair, his face pale, and when he spoke it was very slowly.

'She had lived with me for five years. She was an alcoholic, neurotic and unhappy. Most of her life she'd been unhappy. Her husband is an artist, he lives in County Cork somewhere. I tried to help. It never lasted long, the good bits.'

'Did she ever threaten suicide?'

'Frequently.'

'Any particular reason?'

'She was an unhappy person, no particular reason, just found it hard to be alive.'

'Any idea of her parents' address?'

'Blantyre House, Bray, just outside Dublin.'

'Do they keep in touch with her?'

Mills shook his head wearily.

'Not for the last four years.'

Evans nodded, but his eyes were still on Mills' face.

'How old are you, Mr Mills?'

'Fifty-one.'

'What do you do—your work?'

'I work at an agency—an advertising agency—I'm the creative director.'

'How old was Miss Seymour?'

'Twenty-six, maybe twenty-seven. I'm not sure.'

'What did she do?'

'You mean her work?'

'Yes.'

'She hadn't worked for a long time.'

Evans looked at the younger man, who didn't respond. They both stood up and Evans held out his hand.

'I'm sorry to have added to your worries, Mr Mills. You've been very helpful. It's unlikely that we shall be contacting you again but it's certain that you'll be asked to attend at the inquest.'

When they were in the hall he glanced again, briefly, at the debris on the floor, looked at Mills, opened his mouth as if to speak, then, seemingly thinking better of it, just nodded as they walked into the foyer.

They walked from the block of flats to where their car

was parked near the porters' glass-fronted office. Evans sat in the driving seat, his hand on the ignition key.

'What did you think, Tom?'

'He was speaking the truth all right. The local police have got a stack of complaints about the girl. She's been done twice for drunk in charge and a couple of times for cheque frauds. He must have been bloody stupid to take her on.'

Back at the flat Mills sat in one of the deep armchairs. He'd had to drop the habit of a pre-dinner whisky, and right now he could have done with one. His mind circled round the thought of those troubled green eyes, and the long black hair, as part of a corpse. At the start, for one whole year, she'd stayed on the wagon, but after that the old friends from Ireland had caught up, and then there'd been the dreary routine of bottles in the toilet cistern, in coat pockets, and the dustbin. Even if you had once been in counter-intelligence, a determined alcoholic can beat you by the third week without really trying. And now she'd beaten the world, and the uncaring parents who were embarrassed by their black sheep. You could easily rationalize, and say that it was a merciful release. But the one who got left behind, the one who had failed, had to try and pick up the pieces. Of one thing Mills was quite sure. He'd leave the flat, and its crises and dark nights, maybe he'd leave the job as well.

He had taken a bag to the Coroner's Court and when it was over—'Death by misadventure'—he had hailed a taxi and gone to Heathrow. He had landed at Naples and then taken the bus to Amalfi. But there was no such easy escape, the girl had gone with him, and on beaches and hillsides he'd heard those words again and again. 'I couldn't survive without you, David. I'd never make it.' On the fourth day he flew back to London.

There were four letters awaiting him at the flat. One was from the police at Putney asking for instructions for disposing of the green Mini, which had now been recovered, and was in a nearby garage. It was registered in his name. The second was from the insurance company, pointing out one of the small print clauses that released them from any insurance obligations. The third was addressed to 'Major Mills M.C.' and bore a Dublin postmark. It was from a firm of solicitors in Cork. It was badly typed but the message was clear.

Dear Sir,

Our clients Mr and Mrs Seymour of Blantyre House, Bray, Co. Wicklow, have instructed us in the matter of Miss Jane Seymour deceased.

They wish it to be put on record that they hold you responsible for the events which led up to her death and have instructed us to take advice from Senior Counsel to consider what action they may take in the Courts. In the meantime we have been instructed to arrange for the return of Miss Seymour's belongings from your premises. Will you please forward these by National Carriers to this address.

Yours faithfully,

O'Mahoney, Sullivan and Fletcher

They'd gone to Cork solicitors to keep the scandal out of Dublin. There was nothing they could do, but their hypocrisy went hand in hand with venom.

The fourth letter was very brief. It just asked him to phone a London number as soon as possible. There was no signature, and no address. The postmark was W1. The envelope was buff, overprinted OHMS.

The flat was silent and very still, and he could hear the traffic from Putney Hill. He sat in the armchair and pulled the telephone over to the coffee table in front of him. He looked at the letter, and dialled the number. As he dialled the last digit he realized it was Sunday, and wherever it was would be closed. He was about to replace the receiver when he heard a click, and a voice said 'Duty Officer Foreign Office, can I help you?'

'My name's Mills. David Mills. I was asked to ring this number.'

'What was the subject, Mr Mills?'

'No idea. I just got a note asking me to phone.'

'Just a moment, please.'

There was silence for a couple of minutes and then the same voice came on the line again.

'Putting you through, Mr Mills.'

After the usual clicks and static another voice came on the line.

'David, this is James McHugh.'

'I'm sorry, who?'

'James McHugh. You knew me at 21 Army Group.'

'Of course. Of course. It's been a long time. I'm sorry. I didn't recognize the name after all that time.'

'Of course not, David.' A pause. 'I wondered if we could meet?'

'Sure. I'd like that. When would suit you?'

'How about tonight. Say the Café Royal about eight?'

'OK. In the bar.'

'They've altered it around a bit recently, let's meet in the old bar.'

They were well into their meal when McHugh said casually, 'Any chance of you giving us some time, David?'

'Who's us?'

McHugh smiled. 'I'm still in the old business. We've got a problem. You could help us.'

'What's the problem?'

'I couldn't go into much detail until you were committed. But let me give you a general picture. D'you remember Colonel Munsel? Otto Munsel. The man you arrested in Hildesheim?'

'Yes, of course. I remember him well.'

'He was very co-operative at 21 Army Group, but by some administrative blunder he was left hanging about in the POW cage for nearly two years. In the end he did a bunk. We never caught up with him. Two years later he turned up as a very senior man in the Bonn government offices. He was liaison between the Federal intelligence agencies and the politicians in the Bundestag.

'At the moment we've got a pretty tough problem in Germany. Munsel has been approached for help, but he won't play. He's quite within his official rights of course. Protocol is on his side. But we think he might co-operate with you.'

'What exactly do you want me to do?'

McHugh topped up their glasses, and carefully pushed back his plate so that he could rest his elbows on the table.

'We'd like you to come back in the racket.'

'I'm a bit old for those games.'

'We don't think so. You've got the experience and the contact. You could try this one operation. See how it goes.'

'And if it doesn't work out?'

'You'll have earned more than you can at the advertising agency. It'll be tax free, and if you choose not to stay on you'd be paid till you got fixed up somewhere. And a small pension.'

'How long do you reckon this operation will take?'

'Hard to say, David. A few months maybe.'

'How about I sleep on it?'

'Very sensible. If you decide against it phone me at this number. If you agree, or you want to discuss it, meet me at this address at four tomorrow.' He opened his wallet and pushed a card across the table. There was an address typed on it and a telephone number. It was in a road at the back of Victoria Station.

Number 57 Alma Road could no longer be considered a tribute to the Duke's Peninsular campaigns. The brown paint on the front door stood up in blisters, and in places you could see the original wood. The windows upstairs and downstairs were dusty and flyblown. On the brass plaque the words were just discernible—'The Climax Employment Agency. Licensed by the GLC.' Mills looked for a bell or a door-knocker, but there was none. He tried the big brass door-knob and the door opened grudgingly as he stepped inside. A middle-aged lady sat at a typewriter and looked him over.

'Who did you want, sir?'

'Mr McHugh.'

'Ah yes. Just a moment.'

She lifted a phone, and listened for a few moments. She neither dialled nor spoke, then she replaced the receiver. She smiled a faded smile and pointed to a door behind her.

'Just go through, sir.'

Behind the door was a narrow passage-way with high brick walls. At the far end it turned sharp right, and James McHugh stood at an open door.

'Come on in, David.'

The big metal door swung to, and McHugh turned a brass dial like the combination lock on a safe. He took Mills' arm and turned into a small bright office. There was a small colour TV set, and a communications transceiver on a long shelf. No desk, but a low white circular coffee table, and half-a-dozen leather arm-chairs.

McHugh leaned back and looked across at Mills.

'Well, David, I'm glad you're here.'

'What do we do about my agency contract?'

'Don't worry about that. We'll square that off one way or another. To their benefit, of course. Have you got any other things to clear up?'

'The flat and the furniture, that's all.'

McHugh nodded and lifted the phone. With his finger poised over the dial he held the receiver away from his ear.

'We can do that for you. I was sorry about the girl, David.'

And he dialled two numbers and listened.

'Lambton? Bring me in the files I listed.'

The dark girl who brought in the files didn't glance even for a moment at Mills.

McHugh leaned back in his chair with his feet up on the white table.

'You'll find a fat file on Munsel. We had great respect for him. Co-operated without making a song and dance about it. He was offered a change of nationality by us and by the Yanks. Turned both down without any heroics. Was offered a top job in the Gehlen set-up because of his experience with Foreign Armies East. Reckoned they were dangerous fanatics. Wouldn't touch 'em with a barge pole. He was right of course, they were packed full of Nazis—SS, Gestapo, SD—all the naughty boys who'd operated against the Russians in the war. But give them their due, they did more than anyone else to keep the Soviets on the hop. They were Allan Dulles' favourite boys in Europe, and they got a lot of help from the CIA. Money, information, and political support of course. They made the CIA in Germany look like innocents abroad.

'When the German Government wanted "détente" with Moscow, Willy Brandt got a lot of stick from the Russians about the Gehlen organization, but CIA pressure kept them going. Until Nixon also wanted détente with the Russians, that is. Then they pulled the rug out from under Gehlen's lot. Gehlen retired, and a new guy took over. All the naughty boys got the chop and it was respectable again. And ineffective of course. Spent a lot of its time digging up the dirt on the SPD and feeding it to the opposition. The CIA kept up a vague relationship, but it was less than half-hearted.

'That was the position for about eighteen months. Then six months ago we started getting reports from a number of sources that the old Gehlen organization was in business again. We did some careful checking in Bonn. They obviously knew something but they weren't letting on. Very tactful, very diplomatic, but nothing doing. We had tentative words with CIA liaison and they were categorical, even touches of indignation here and there. We got the impression that it was genuinely the first they'd heard of a revival, but we also got the impression that they liked the sound of it. A month ago our ambassador in Moscow was given two pages of text. Shoved in his hand at a reception. When it was translated it turned out to be a report of an investigation that the KGB had done in Sofia on sabotage.

'Three factories outside Sofia had been severely damaged by explosions. Several workers were killed. In a matter of hours the rumour was around that it had been done by the KGB. It was claimed that the KGB's intention was to teach the Romanian Government that they'd better stick close to the Moscow line—or else. The Sofia papers, and all the rest of them, hotly denied the charges, but nobody could offer a credible alternative. The KGB report was very specific. You'll find it in the files. They said it had been done by a group of ex-Gehlen men. It fits in with our picture.'

McHugh looked across at Mills as if inviting a comment.

'When did the Gehlen organization close down?'

'Gehlen retired in May 1968, and a General Wessel took over. He re-organized it, but it became pretty useless. Then when Willy Brandt and the Social Democrats came in after the 1970 election there was another purge, and that's when all the former SS and Gestapo men were clobbered. The group heads were nearly all replaced by Social Democrats. The West Germans preferred it that way—the government, and the public in general. The CIA screamed like stuck pigs. They had good reason to. A big chunk of their intelligence apparatus had been ripped apart. When the CIA were getting frantic to see Kruschev's speech to the presidium denouncing Stalin it was Gehlen who got it for them. Complete, and in four days flat. Their organization inside the Warsaw Pact countries was first-class at all levels.'

'Tell me about Otto Munsel.'

'He's entirely non-political for a start. His job is to hold the ring between the politicians and the services so far as security is concerned. The internal security of the Federal Republic—nothing else. Keeps well in the background.

Respected by all the political parties, and his mates in the services. Very small staff, he's not operative in any way. He collects the various intelligence reports and analyses situations. If he was more ambitious he'd extend himself as a trouble-shooter but he doesn't. He sticks to the rules and goes right down the middle. Teaches the politicians and the soldiers how to translate one another.'

'And you think he will co-operate with me?'

McHugh smiled wryly. 'Far from it. All we know is, that he certainly won't co-operate with anyone else.'

'Is he that important?'

'Well, let's put it like this. If he was on our side, the most he could do is point us in the right direction. You'll see from the files that there is a reasonable amount of evidence of a revival of ex-Gehlen operations. But we've no names, no addresses, no leads. Almost all the information is isolated. It never links, it doesn't appear to overlap, and a lot of it comes from uncheckable sources in East Germany or the Soviet Union.'

'What's the Soviet attitude?'

McHugh looked over his glasses grinning. 'They were making some headway. We heard that they had made at least one contact, and then their friends in East Germany planted their man on Willy Brandt. When that fell apart and Brandt resigned, the German security service got a lot of stick, and they broke up a lot of the Warsaw Pact networks. At the moment it seems they're stuck. I expect that's why they've been pushing stuff our way, to see if we'll do their dirty work for them.'

'And what's the official view?'

'Oh, that's quite clear. We don't like private armies. Anything we can't control is dangerous. These sort of boys would start World War III if they got the chance. The Americans share our views. Officially anyway. The CIA are still recovering from the Nixon scandals, and a new scandal could finish them. The State Department and the White House are as one on this. They want it stopped before it gets out of hand.'

'Will they co-operate?'

'Sure they will. They're sending a top man over. He's worked in a variety of areas. A chap they've used before as a troubleshooter. They are not sure of where the CIA support for this new group lies. Their man will report direct to the CIA deputy director.'

McHugh stood up slowly, and stretched his arms. 'The files are there for you, David. There are living quarters here and we'd like you to stay here for two or three days while we extricate you and make a few arrangements. Miss Ames will get you anything you want including money. Make yourself at home.'

Mills had sat for a long time, staring at the brown and red files, but making no move to look at them. He felt suddenly lonely. But it was a strangely comfortable loneliness, like prison or the army. The past didn't seem to exist any more, in this sparsely furnished room.

Chapter 9

In one of the side bays at Dallas International Airport, two men stood outside a wooden hut, looking up into the evening sky. One was wearing a pale blue light-weight suit, and the other wore khaki drill and a yellow silk scarf. He was shading his eyes as he watched a small plane at about a thousand feet, doing figures of eight, waiting for the control tower to let him down.

The man with the scarf said slowly, 'Yes, I guess that's Pierce all right. The wing tips are different from the old Cherokee and that cabin looks bigger. Wonder what's keeping him.'

Up in the Piper PA-28-180 the pilot was wearing a plastic headset with one phone on his ear, and the other pushed back as he listened to control. Control were trying to check the position of a Mexican pilot who had lost his way and wandered over the border into Texas. They were hampered by the fact that he couldn't speak much English.

'Can you see any water—lakes or rivers?'

'No—not see no water.'

'Can you describe what you can see?'

'Not see nothing.'

'Jesus. Let's go back. Where did you start from?'

'Nuevo Laredo.'

'And where were you going?'

'Monterrey.'

'OK. Keep circling, we'll be back to you.'

They went on half-power, and the pilot of the Cherokee looked down at his maps. As he looked he guessed what the Mexican had done, he'd gone off up the reciprocal bearing. Should have been on a south-west bearing of about 200° and he'd headed north-east on around 20°. He'd been spotted at San Antonio forty minutes earlier, so now he must be right in the Fort Worth-Dallas complex. Some instinct made the pilot look up and out to his right. He laughed and switched to transmit on the control tower frequency.

'Control tower from Cherokee.'

'Sorry, pilot, we've got an emergency, you'll have to wait where we've put you.'

'He's out over Grapevine Reservoir, control. You can see him. About 27°.'

There was a crackle of static, and control came back. 'Thanks, pilot, we'll get him down first. You'll be next and you have instructions to taxi to Bay nine.'

Pierce Rochford III was a slim wiry fellow, not too big, looked a bit like Richard Widmark. It was something about the mouth and the eyes, or maybe the scar down the side of his face, a souvenir from Korea. The Rochford clan were Texans and the money had come from lumber. Pierce Rochford III had put a large part of his fortune into property. In property development there are long waits, while Federal authorities, mayors, and the Mafia, decide whether you can do what you plan to do, and how much of the action they want for saying the magic word. This means long periods of waiting around, and Pierce Rochford III filled these gaps in his business life tinkering with planes and pretty girls. But from time to time he got calls from old friends who needed help. The special sort of help that an ex-CIA man, who moves in the right circles, can give more easily than an outsider. With cars the experts say that there's no substitute for litres, and in some influential circles there's no substitute for money. Old, old money. CIA money would be spotted a mile away.

The two men were waiting for him, and they took him to the wooden building at the edge of the bay. Inside it was comfortable, and the air-conditioning was working.

They didn't spend much time on chit-chat because Pierce Rochford's charm didn't come from small-talk. He started the ball rolling himself as he leaned back and loosened his collar and tie.

'You guys want something?'

It was the older man in the khaki drill who put down his drink. 'You remember that job you did for us in Germany?'

'You mean at Pullach?'

'Yes.'

Rochford said no more and the older man looked intently at the thin pale face and the watchful grey eyes.

'You know what happened in the end?'

'I know Gehlen retired and that the outfit's run now by the German government.'

'No more than that, Pierce?'

Rochford shook his head. 'No, general—no more than that.'

The man in the blue suit cleared his throat and the older man turned to him. 'Tell him, Jake, put him in the picture.'

'We've had a report from the British that a group of ex-Nazis from the old Gehlen outfit have set up their own organization. Fanatically anti-Soviet, and beginning to be effective. They've got connections in England, France and the States, and they've got a strong network in Germany—both sides of the border. We'd like you to have a look at it for us. They're rocking the boat, Pierce, and they're dangerous.'

'Why not get the CIA to do it?'

The other two men exchanged glances and the older man leaned back in his chair. Neither of them spoke for a few moments, and then the older man said.

'There's an indication that some of their funds come from CIA. Maybe not, but right now the indications are that they get funds and information from the CIA.'

'What have we got on these guys then?'

'Not much. The British have got a bit and you'd be working with one of their men from SIS.'

Rochford looked at them both, and then slowly stood up, looking at his watch.

'How long do you reckon this will take?'

'Hard to say, Pierce. Three or four months maybe.'

'Where's the dope on them?'

The general nodded towards the trestle table. There were six or seven thin files and a film can.

'It's all there, Pierce. Including a report on the SIS guy you'd be working with.'

'You got a phone here?'

The general pointed to a phone on a bracket on the far wall. Rochford dialled a number and arranged for his plane to be fuelled, and the tyres checked. Still holding the phone he said. 'I'm taking a girl to Acapulco for the weekend. Where'll you be on Monday?'

'Usual number in Washington. This mean you'll do it?'

Rochford nodded. 'You'll have funds and the gear ready by then?'

The general smiled. 'They're ready now, fella.'

Mills had explored the small but comfortable flat, Miss Ames had provided a simple meal, and then he had got down to the files.

There was a long report on the old Gehlen organization with an appendix on Fremde Heere Ost. The original 21 Army Group interrogation of Munsel had been cut down to forty pages. That too was mainly about FHO. There were reports from over thirty sources covering the period from his escape from the PW cage to a recent conference in Bonn. He lived just outside Bonn with his family. The son was married with a daughter of his own, aged two. Munsel's daughter was twenty, a student at Göttingen University. There were vague references to Munsel's involvement with a young woman, and a number of indications that his relationship with the Count, his father-in-law, was chilly or maybe non-existent. An asssesment of his work categorized it as efficient and thorough, but not spectacular. There were several reports that both the SPD and the CDU had offered him party seats in the Bundesrat. His hobbies were given as riding and sailing, but he belonged to no clubs. His wife Helga worked hard for the Karitas Verband, a Roman Catholic charity, and had a small circle of friends with whom she played bridge. They had no social round, and neither of them attended even official parties.

There was a separate report on past relationships between the Gehlen organization and the CIA, covering finance and technical aid. As an appendix was an outline of the structure, and financing by the CIA, of Radio Free Europe and Radio Liberty.

Finally, there was a thin file of all the material that had been gathered, that indicated that a new, clandestine version of the Gehlen organization might exist. There was a long list of over three hundred names of ex-Nazis dismissed from the Gehlen group with reference numbers to personal files where they existed. A six-page report gave details of conversations with Federal Government officials, including three Ministers. They were all inconclusive. An SIS situation report merely drew attention to various minor events that had occurred in Warsaw pact countries in the last six months. There was a pattern of embarrassment to the Soviets that had caused friction with their satellite allies. The material from the KGB drew attention to sabotage of factories, railways and a radio station. The incidents were in Poland, Yugoslavia and Romania. Attached to the KGB report was a photostated copy of an item in *The Times*. It was by-lined by Gabriel Ronay and Mills read it through carefully.

MOSCOW DENIES ROMANIA SABOTAGE

Pravda has angrily rejected Bucharest rumours alleging secret Soviet involvement in a series of devastating fires and explosions which have crippled a number of key industrial plants in Romania.

The newspaper insisted that neither the Soviet Union nor any of its Warsaw pact allies had anything to do with the fires and, in its traditional West-baiting tone, claimed that western reports of the alleged sabotage acts were yet another attempt to create tension in the Balkans.

But *Pravda* did not say that the rumoured explosions resulting in heavy loss of life were without foundation.

After a long silence, and perhaps understandable hesitation, the Romanian Communist Party newspaper *Scinteia* has now confirmed that fires and explosions have indeed taken place in a number of industrial plants.

But it did so in order to deny with all the authority at its disposal that disaffected Transylvanian-Hungarians, allegedly operating with Soviet support, were behind the mysterious explosions in the oil and petrochemical industries.

McHugh had joined him at breakfast-time the next morning. He was holding a thin brown file. As he sat down he put it on the floor beside his chair.

'That's the file on Pierce Rochford, David. The Americans have already agreed that it's to be an SIS operation. You'll be in charge but Rochford will cover any USA liaison you need. He's ex-CIA, knows the ropes, and he's got plenty of experience. A likeable chap; if you have any problems in that area let me know right away. You've got to keep in mind that it's almost certain that some part of the CIA is funding this break-away group. You'll be the number one target if they get a smell of what you're up to. And remember, they're high-up enough to channel large chunks of CIA money to these boys, expecting to get away with it—they're defying White House instructions, and they're not going to give a damn about eliminating anybody who gets in the way.'

'Are you quite sure that Rochford is safe?'

McHugh leaned back with a shrug of his shoulders. 'How can I be sure? The people he will report to are trusted completely by the White House, they in turn have picked Rochford. We've done a bit of checking too, there are no grounds for doubting. Not yet anyway. But I'll say it again, if you have any doubts, at any stage, then tell me—right away.'

'OK. When does Rochford arrive?'

'He's here. We're giving you the safe house in Ebury Street and . . .' he looked at his watch, 'he should be there by now.' He looked across at Mills. 'Shall we go across there?'

When McHugh let them into the flat, Rochford was sitting relaxed in a deep armchair and a drink in his hand. His tie was on the arm of the chair and there was a record playing on the hi-fi. It was Frankie singing 'Second Time Around' and Rochford seemed more interested in hearing the last few bars than meeting the new arrivals.

Then, as McHugh walked across the room, Rochford swung his skinny legs to the floor and stood up. He was smiling, and he held out his hand.

'Good to see you again, Mac. How's that pretty daughter making out?'

'She's fine, Pierce. Nearly fourteen now so you haven't got long to wait. This is David Mills.'

The shrewd grey eyes took him in for only a split second before Rochford swung round and gripped his hand.

'Glad to know you, David. Have you seen this guy's little gal?'

'Fraid I haven't.'

'By Jesus she's a honey—a real doll, and does she know it. Going to be a killer when she grows up.'

They had sat and talked of mutual friends for half an hour. Then McHugh got down to business.

'Any news your side, Pierce?'

The alert eyes were squinting at the fresh drink that he

lifted to the light. He spoke without looking at either of them.

'Well, I'll tell you this, the General's taking your stuff very seriously.' He put down the glass and then leaned back holding out his hand palm upwards, with the fingers outstretched as he pointed at them in turn.

'He's cut me out from reporting to, one, anybody on the 40 Committee, including the chairman; two, the Director of Clandestine operations, Western Hemisphere; three, the Office of Policy Co-ordination. So he's taking it seriously all right.'

'Have you got any views yourself, Pierce?'

The neat head went back and rested on the chair, looking up at the ceiling.

'You guys heard of "The Farm"?'

'Is that the training place at Williamsburg?'

'That's it, Mac. That's the place. Seemed to me to be worth a look for this type of operation.' He turned and looked at Mills.

'You know this outfit, David?'

Mills shook his head.

'Well, let me tell ya. It's a CIA training facility, mainly used by Clandestine Operations. One of their special scenarios is a section for training border crossers. They've got a whole big patch, all set up as a simulated closed border. Covers twenty miles or so, and there's all the usual stuff, checkpoints, mines, electronics—the lot. I thought it might be worth doing a check on current activity there.' The lean face creased in a grin. 'I didn't get anywhere near it. It was all wrapped up very tight. And that's not normal.'

He took another slug of his drink. 'So I wandered off course in the Cherokee the next day. Took the General with me as ballast. Filed a flight plan from Washington to Newport News. When we got off course they sent up a chopper. When they found the General was on board they escorted us back to Highway 64 with full courtesies. I got some pictures as we crossed "The Farm". I've got them here. The main mock-up is the check-point at Helmstedt. I'd guess from the number of bodies moving around that they've got a pretty full training programme going on. The guy who specializes on the East German border is Larry Polanski. He's an old pal of mine from way back. I phoned his wife and she said Larry had left the CIA four months ago. Seems like he's gone into the import-export business. Guess where?'

He lit a cigarette and inhaled before he looked across at them. 'West Germany is where. She didn't know what he traded in and she ain't seen hide nor hair of him for three months. Had letters in that time, postmarked Hanover, Berlin, Hamburg and London. She filed a petition for divorce just after he left CIA, quoting mental cruelty and non-cohabitation. A week later she got a visit from a guy named John G. Makin. He's the personal smoothie of the Director of Plans.' Rochford stubbed out his cigarette and turned to Mills. 'That's the current cover, David, for Clandestine Operations. Anyway, John G. explained that she was due a special separation allowance of a thousand bucks a month, and hinted that Larry still had connections. He'd brought a cheque with him for three months' payments and Julie took the hint and withdrew the petition. Seems like John G. sees her week-ends to keep her happy. She's happy with John G. and I'd guess the extra bread looks after the rest of the week.'

Rochford stood up and stretched. 'If the boys wanted to play games with the alumni of the Gehlen outfit, Larry Polanski would be on the team. There's nothing conclusive out of all this, but I'd rate it as a strong indication.'

'Sounds like they *have* got CIA backing. And at a high level.'

'So where do we go? How about this guy Otto Munsel?'

'I'll contact him in the next few days, and see what I can fish up.' Mills looked at McHugh. 'Any reason why Pierce shouldn't come too?'

McHugh shook his head. 'None that I can see. Maybe you should see him on your own the first time. Just so that it doesn't look too official. I'll get on my way now and leave you two to get on with it. Let me know, David, what you want in money and facilities. There'll be no problem there.'

Chapter 10

Even on a good day the airfield at Wahn looks grey and lonely, and as the plane's wing dipped, they came round in a wide circle over the dark pine forests. Wahn had been a Luftwaffe airfield, and its grim, inaccessible site, thirty-seven kilometres from Bonn, had never been a happy posting, and now, thirty-five years later, it served Bonn and Cologne with no great effort to impress visitors. Mills and Rochford took a taxi and booked in at the Königshof.

The big, wide windows looked over the Rhine, and as Rochford bathed Mills stood at the window and watched the traffic on the wide, brown-coloured river. The long trains of barges shouldered their way down the main channel with their loads of pig-iron or coal, and even their dirty cargoes looked neat and clean in the summer sun. There were pleasure steamers with striped awnings, and a mother and baby sitting on the bright green bank, waving to every boat that passed. For just a brief moment the orderliness, the peacefulness, seemed to Mills a sickening contrast with what was really going on. The deception and double deceptions that led to more and more repressions, till war looked an easy escape from the massive tangle of intrigue and pressures. Maybe Karl Marx was right and the serfs didn't really mind their serfdom if they got as good a deal from their lord and master as the next baron gave to *his* slaves. Communism, democracy, the labels that politicians gave to whatever kept them in power, maybe it didn't matter, and never had, to most of their countrymen. They just wanted to be left alone to get on with their lives. But it was those rosy labels that gave men the excuse to keep the world on edge. Give a man a flag and you could teach him to hate. He shook his head like a dog coming out of water and walked to the door.

The taxi-driver knew the address but didn't like the drive. It was nine kilometres, just beyond Bad Godesberg. As the taxi pulled away Mills looked at the high walls and the wrought-iron gates. There was a gravel path leading up through a tree-lined walk of chestnuts and beeches to the big white house. As he closed the gate he could see stone vases hung with bright red geraniums and lobelia, lining a patio that gave on to the back of the house. There were vines, he saw, as he approached, and already there were bunches of small green grapes hanging in the delicate pellucid light from the late sun. Two men sat talking, unaware of him as he approached. They sat at a white circular table with a bottle of pale wine between them. The man on the left was leaning forward, arms on the table, moving his head vigorously to emphasize what he was saying. The man on the right was relaxed and smiling, looking at his drink as he swung the pale liquid in the wide glass. The man on the right was Otto Munsel. As Mills' foot scraped on the bottom step leading to the patio, Munsel turned his head sharply, the smile fading. He stood up, and drink in hand he walked over towards Mills.

'Darf ich Ihnen helfen, mein Freund? Haben Sie vielleicht . . . My God, my God, it's Mills—Captain Mills. This is wonderful, what brings you here?' Without waiting for an answer he clasped Mills' hand and turned to the other man. 'Gottfried, this is Captain Mills, the Englishman I have told you about.' Then he turned back to Mills, smiling his obvious pleasure, looking over his face. He opened his mouth to speak, then hesitated, and as the other man walked across he said 'Let me introduce you, David. This is Regierungsrat Hummel, he is one of the advisers to the Government on transport. Wants us to go back to horses to save oil.'

The Regierungsrat was a big stocky man and he offered

a firm hard hand to Mills, but there was no great enthusiasm in his eyes. He looked old enough, and tough enough, to have gone in the bag for something or other in 1945.

Munsel hurried into the house calling his wife, and after a few moments' silence Hummel nodded at Mills. 'I'll be on my way Herr Hauptmann. Please tell Otto that I'll call him tomorrow. No doubt you'll have much to talk about together. Auf Wiedersehen.' He crunched off down the gravel path and through a stand of young birches, heading for some side exit from the grounds.

Then Munsel was back. His wife was grey-haired now and her face was thin, but somehow she looked handsome. More handsome than she had looked as a girl. She too was smiling, and the welcome was real, and warm. A lot must have happened since that day, long ago, when she had said her cold little 'thank you' speech.

A manservant brought out a tray of glasses and two bottles of champagne. As Munsel popped the first fat cork, he said over his shoulder, 'So tell me, David, what are you doing here in the Bundesrepublik? Whatever it is we send up our thanks.' As the champagne foamed into the glasses Mills waited till Munsel sat down. 'I came to see you, Otto.' Munsel looked up quickly, almost apprehensively. 'Cheers, David. What a terrible host to ask why you're here. You're here and that's all that matters. Tell us what you've been doing all these years.'

'For the last fourteen or fifteen years I've been in advertising. Copy-writing, then director of an agency. Nothing exciting, nothing special.'

'Are you married?'

'No. Came near it a few times but never finally got there.'

'But plenty of girls I suspect, Captain Mills.' Helga was looking female and knowing.

'One at a time, Helga, never more. And what about you two? You've got a family. One I know of for sure but I seem to remember another name on a Christmas card—a girl's name?'

'Yes, Gerhard was saved from disgrace by your kindness. He's a doctor now and doing well. He is a consultant on the heart for the big centre in Hanover. Has a small girl of his own. Nice wife, and all very happy and *comme il faut.*'

Munsel poured out more champagne and Mills had a feeling that he was avoiding the subject of the daughter.

'And the girl—your daughter?'

'Ah, well. She's very pretty, David. *Typisch deutsch,* blonde hair, blue eyes and all the rest of it. Went to the University at Göttingen for a couple of terms. Wasn't academic really. A mistake. She's back home with us now.'

There was a moment's silence and then Helga Munsel spoke. 'You know, Captain Mills, what I really owe you is my husband. Those few days you gave him of his life made much difference. Not just at that time but always. You made him believe in people again. Gave him strength and calmness. We owe very much to you. Whenever we came to England I always wanted to contact you but Otto said, "No. We shall all meet again when it is time." He was right—as always.' She smiled at the two men. 'We have told the children so much about you. You are a sort of legend in this family. The knight in shining armour.' Mills smiled and the handsome woman shook her head. 'No. You must not laugh. We are very serious about it.'

Then Munsel interrupted. 'David, you'll eat with us, won't you?'

'If you invite me.' He smiled.

Munsel stood up. 'No. No invitations. This is your home when you're in Germany.'

Then, as they all stood awkwardly at this expression of sentiment a girl came round from the side of the house. She was holding a tennis racket and was dressed in a thin white sweater and a pair of tight shorts. The blonde hair was long, well below her shoulders, and the pert nose gave on to a wide soft mouth that showed her white healthy teeth. She looked a very young twenty, except for the two full breasts that stretched her sweater, and the big blue eyes. They were big like the eyes in a statue, and they looked at him from the first moment with awareness and invitation. There was a moment's silence, and then Munsel said, 'Jutta, meet David Mills.'

The girl looked at him, as she held out her hand she smiled, and the teeth set off the soft redness of her lips. Her eyes looked into his, amused, confident of her beauty, and her nostrils had flared almost imperceptibly as she said, 'Welcome Mr Mills. I used to be told about you instead of Hans Anderson.'

And they were all at ease again. They talked politics and music all through dinner, and then the girl and her mother left them. When the table had been cleared Munsel leaned forward with his arms folded on the table.

'So tell me, David. Why are you here? Can you tell me? My instinct says it's politics of some sort.'

'Can I speak in confidence, Otto?'

'Absolutely. When you get to dangerous ground I'll tell you.'

'I need your advice.'

He waited, but Munsel was silent, his face impassive.

'We're worried about the old Gehlen organization.'

'The Gehlen organization doesn't exist any more. It's the BND now, fully under control of the Federal Chancellery. No Nazis that we know of and a straightforward operation.'

'Agreed. It's some of the Nazis who used to be in Gehlen's outfit who concern us.'

'They were dismissed or retired years ago.'

'We think they may still be working. Outside the Gehlen set-up. Nothing to do with the BND.'

Munsel moved an empty coffee cup around.

'Where would they get the funds?'

'Nazi sympathizers?'

Munsel shook his head. 'No chance. Old Nazis are either broke or very rich. If they're broke they don't have funds. If they're rich they aren't going to take any risks. Our tax authorities can probe every penny.'

'What about the CIA?'

Munsel was shuffling crumbs on the tablecloth and he didn't look up as he spoke. 'You mean the American Government would take that risk?'

'No, not the government. Just the CIA, or part of the CIA. The part that stopped getting any intelligence out of the Soviets when Gehlen was finished?'

Munsel leaned back slowly and looked across at Mills as if weighing him up.

'I suppose that's possible.'

'Have you heard any rumours on the subject?'

Munsel reached forward. 'More coffee, David?'

Mills didn't reply.

'In Bonn there are rumours every hour. Most of them are true.'

'Is this rumour true?'

Munsel shifted on his chair and pushed it to face the window.

'David, I can't make any more comment. Whatever our relationship I would be going against my duty. Maybe you tell me what you are here to do.'

'The British Government and the American Government believe this is going on. They want to stop it right now. I've been told to do that. I came for your help or advice.'

'Help I certainly can't give you. Advice maybe. But you may not like it.'

'Try me.'

'Leave it to us to deal with this.'

Mills shook his head. 'That would have to be between governments. They wouldn't discuss it—even hypothetically. Your people wouldn't want to admit that it exists and that they can't stop it. The Americans wouldn't agree for a moment that part of the CIA was contravening White House instructions, and my government wouldn't risk being accused of doing the KGB's dirty work for them. It's unofficial or nothing.'

Munsel nodded. 'You go and talk to the ladies for a while, and I'll make a phone call or two. I'll see what can be done. But I'm not optimistic. I can only hint to them and I am sure the answer will be negative.'

'Where are they? The ladies.'

'Helga will be gathering flowers maybe. Even in the dark she does it.'

Mills walked over to the patio. Across the lush green lawns there were beds of flowers lit by yellow lights, and where the lawns sloped away, a summer-house and a half-circle of trees were bathed in white floodlight so that their leaves sparkled like jewels in the evening breeze. The grass was damp with dew as he walked slowly across the springy turf. There was the English smell of mown grass and the humid tropical odour of lush foliage from ferns and shrubs. When he thought that he heard voices from the summer-house he turned back up the slope in that direction. The light from the nearby trees flooded the canopy of the white-painted wooden structure and illuminated the inside like bright moonlight. The light made a halo round the girl's blonde hair. The linen straps of the white dress she had worn for dinner had been pulled down from her shoulders and she watched as the man's hands cupped her breasts. The man was Gottfried Hummel, and he was too intent on what he was doing to notice Mills. But as if by some instinct the girl looked towards him. For a moment he thought she couldn't see him and then he saw her mocking smile as the man fondled her avidly. Even when his hand smoothed her flat young belly and slid down to her thighs she stood smiling as he fondled her before she turned and, speaking quietly, said something that made him smile as she slid back the shoulder straps of her dress. Mills had stood as if hypnotized and then he had turned and walked away silently, back to the house.

Munsel was smoking a cigar and suddenly he looked very German and defensive. As soon as he saw Mills he stood up. He shook his head. 'There was a brick wall, David.' He shrugged. 'It was a mistake to ask. Now I cannot help you in any way.'

'It doesn't matter, Otto. I really didn't expect any help. Not official help anyway. I really wanted your opinion, and, if I were lucky, your advice.'

Munsel stubbed out the half-smoked cigar. Mills realized he was playing for time. Time to make up his mind about something. Finally he leaned back and spoke with his eyes closed. His voice low, almost a whisper.

'Do you remember when we went up to Glücksburg all those years ago?'

'Of course.'

'You remember what we were looking for?'

'The records of Fremde Heere Ost.'

Munsel nodded. His eyes still closed.

'Then think about that all over again.' And he stood up suddenly as if galvanized by what he had said.

'Where are you staying, David?'

'At the Königshof. I'll get a taxi.'

'Of course not. I'll drive you in.'

'I must say goodbye to Helga and Jutta.'

'I think Helga's gone to bed. God knows where Jutta will be.'

Mills was aware of the fissures in this family. Munsel's assurance seemed to have suddenly evaporated.

On the way back to Bonn they'd talked of the time just after the war and Munsel's escape from the Interrogation Centre. There was no reference to his influential father-in-law and Mills didn't raise the subject. He was invited to the house the next day if he were going to be available. It was when Mills stood with Munsel on the steps of the hotel that Munsel said quietly, 'Will you still be going ahead with this business?'

Mills nodded.

'I say with only friendship, David. Please be careful, very careful, such people are animals whether they are Germans or Americans. There will be no mercy.'

* * *

Pierce Rochford III was sitting in the bar with a pretty girl. Mills took the key to their room and Rochford had grinned at the girl. 'There, I told you, honey. I'm sleeping with a guy tonight.' The girl looked shocked and then the penny dropped. 'He just your friend.'

'That's it, honey, we're just good friends.' It wasn't much more than half an hour later when Rochford came up to their room.

'How d'ya make out with him, fella?'

'Officially no dice. Temperature freezing. Between the lines, it exists all right. He knows something about it but he isn't telling. But it was clear from a dozen things he said, or left unsaid, that it's going on and they can't stop it.'

'Maybe now Willy Brandt's gone they don't want to stop it.'

'Could be.'

It was just after midday when the girl had phoned. Mills had just hung up from speaking to McHugh in London. She said she wanted to see him that day, and he'd finally been persuaded to pick her up at the inn by the bridge at Bad Godesberg. Rochford had gone to the American Embassy to phone Washington, and Mills sat on the bed thinking about the girl. The voice had been very gentle with an appealing little quaver as she ended each sentence. She had sounded very young and frightened. Probably wondered if he was going to tell Daddy about the scene in the summer-house.

It was just after six o'clock that evening when he walked into the beam-encrusted bar. She was sitting at a table drinking a Coke, and two young men were talking to her. She sat there intent on her drink, paying little attention to the boys. Then she saw him, grabbed her small linen bag, and rushed over to him.

'You're five minutes late.'

'It's not my town, Jutta. Made a few wrong turns.'

'Oh,' she said, not really appeased. 'Where's your car?'

'Right outside.'

'Let's go then.'

'Where shall we go?'

'I'll give you directions.'

The directions ended at the edge of a wood and the girl said, 'Let's find somewhere to sit.' She stopped at a fallen beech tree and perched on the smooth green trunk. The big blue eyes looked at him as she spoke. 'You made my father very unhappy yesterday and I don't understand why. He always said such nice things about you. He always said you were his idea of a civilized man. So what has gone wrong for my father?'

'Nothing's wrong for your father, Jutta. I wanted some help but because of his official position he couldn't help me. I understand that very well. So there's nothing wrong.'

'So why did my father walk about all night. Not sleeping at all. Not all night.'

'Maybe he was worried about something else. You perhaps.'

She looked at him and smiled. 'You are thinking of Herr Hummel, yes?'

'Maybe.'

'But all men like to do that with girls.'

'All men are not your father's friends.'

She shrugged and laughed. 'His friends are the same as other men. They all like to do these things.'

'And you let them?'

Another shrug. 'Why not?'

'What happened at the University?'

'My father did not tell you?'

'He said you were not an academic and that you left after two terms.'

'They dismissed me, I didn't leave. Said I caused trouble with men. He's very disappointed in me, my father. All my life he is disappointed in me and happy about my brother. He is the clever one, the good one.'

And suddenly Mills saw the jig-saw fall into place. The

father with high standards. The son who reflected all this and the daughter who didn't. But the pretty face and the lithe young body squared things off. The important friends of her father, officials and politicians, were offered, and eagerly took, the casual sexual excitements. And for the girl, it would teach her father the facts of life. The fine friends wanted *her*. The pretty face, the exciting breasts, the long shapely legs were more important than the high-flown discussions. It was a subconscious revenge on his judgement of her. His friends voted for her behind his back.

He looked at the girl. A shaft of sunlight brushed the golden hair and lit her face. It was achingly beautiful and the slender neck was smooth and firm. His eyes went to the jutting breasts and as he looked back at her face she was smiling, head on one side with one eye half-closed against the beam of sunlight.

'You would like I take off my sweater?'

He looked at her face for a moment then shook his head. 'There's no need, honey. I'm impressed already.'

'You do not find me beautiful?'

'You're beautiful all right. So are Ming vases and race-horses but I don't need to touch one to prove it.'

She pushed back the long blonde hair so that it coiled over her shoulder. There were two red spots on her cheeks and she looked young and vulnerable. She swung the long legs idly, like a small child.

'What did you ask my father that he could not help you with?'

He held out his hand to her. 'How about I take you to dinner?'

She shrugged and held out her arms like a French girl. 'Lovely, but I'm not dressed for dinner.'

He looked at the tight white sweater and the skin-stretched white jeans and he couldn't imagine any maitre d' refusing her entry.

As they edged their way slowly through Bad Godesberg he saw a florist's and stopped the car. When he hurried back he gave her the furled cornet of pink tissue paper and started the car. When they were out on the main road to Bonn he turned briefly to look at her. She was holding the long-stemmed red rose with both hands, its open bloom just touching her lips. It was the fat tears on her cheek that made him drive into the lay-by and stop. He turned in his seat to look at her but she just looked ahead.

'What's the matter? It was meant to please you.'

She swallowed and then said in a thin unconfident voice, 'It did please me. It did. But it made me sad.'

'Red roses are meant to make pretty girls happy not sad.'

'I know that. I know that.' She paused and then turned to look at him. 'This is the first flower that any man has given me.' She sniffed and felt for a handkerchief. 'My father was right. You are a special man.' Then she grinned. 'A civilized man.'

They had eaten together with Pierce Rochford, and the girl had been amused and cheered by the American's experienced flattery. He drove the girl back to the gates of the house and when he moved to kiss her goodbye the long shapely arms went round his neck and the soft mouth moved on his, and she whispered 'Touch me, David. Touch me like the others do. Show me you like me.' He touched his forehead to hers. 'Jutta, you're beautiful and desirable but that's only half the story. If I did it, it would be very exciting, I wouldn't ever forget it, and that might be bad for both of us.'

Her hand touched his face and she opened the car door. 'If I can help you I will, David. I like saying your name.' And then she was gone.

Back in their room at the hotel Pierce was sitting with two whiskies. He pushed one across for Mills. When Rochford put down his empty glass he said, 'That babe's real dynamite, David.' And he didn't look amused or envious.

'In what way?'

'She's pretty and she's a nympho, and that's a bad combination, fella.'

'What makes you think she's a nympho?'

Rochford lit a cigarette. 'I don't think so, I know so. Every man in the restaurant was panting for her and she'd have taken on the lot.'

'Well, it's not our problem, Pierce.'

'Ho ho. The cool English gentleman stuff. And don't be too darn sure it isn't going to be our problem. She's after you, sonny boy. Grey hair or no grey hair. That pretty little gal's had more men than you've had hamburgers. You're the kind who buy's 'em candies and kisses 'em on the cheek. With these girls that's like laying an aniseed trail for a pack of hounds. Give her a quick bang and she'll drop you and then you'll live to screw another day.'

'Anything from Washington?'

Rochford grinned. 'They suggested we offer Munsel a money deal if you thought he was in the market. I told them it wasn't on.'

'What's the least we need to know, Pierce, to get us started.'

As Rochford opened his mouth to speak the phone rang. There was music in the background and voices. It sounded like a night-club. And then the girl spoke, she was whispering.

'David, can you hear me?'

'Yes. I can hear you.'

'I've found out something to help you.'

He didn't speak. Just waited.

'Are you there, David?'

'Yes.'

'The man you want is called Lerner. Max Lerner. He has a stamp-shop in Hamburg.'

'How do you know this?'

'Father told me.'

'Why?'

'I told him about you and the rose. He just sat there in his study looking very grim. Then he just said, "Tell him

I have heard that it's an old friend of his. Max Lerner. And he's in the stamp business in Hamburg." '

'Where are you now?'

'At the inn.'

'It's nearly two o'clock.'

She laughed. 'It's a private party.' She paused. 'David?'

'Yes.'

'Have I helped?'

'I'm sure you have but I want you to forget all about it. Me, the name, the lot.'

'I love you, David.'

'Honey, I'm old enough to be your father. I like you very much but you ought to be in bed.'

'I'll be right over.'

He laughed despite himself. 'Goodnight, Jutta dear,' and he hung up.

Rochford was pouring another drink for them.

'And what was all that love scene about?'

'*That* was the least we need to know.'

'I don't get it.'

'Her father gave her a man's name to pass on to me.'

'Jesus. What's the name?'

'Lerner. Max Lerner and he's got a stamp shop in Hamburg. Munsel implied that I knew him but I don't. I've never been to Hamburg since the end of the war.'

'You mean a post-office?'

'No, he's a dealer in foreign stamps.'

'How about you check him out on your records and I'll do the same on ours.'

An hour later they turned in.

By ten o'clock the next morning Rochford had received a 'nil report' from Washington on Lerner. Just before noon a Queen's Messenger brought a wax-sealed package for Mills. He ripped it open. There was a one-page typed report, several photographs and some photocopies of newspaper cuttings and documents. He read through the report carefully and half way through he laughed out loud. Rochford looked up from his writing.

'What's the comedy script?'

'It's the SIS report on Max Lerner.' He looked up grinning. 'He was arrested in a small dump called Glücksburg in 1945.'

Rochford looked unimpressed. 'So what.'

'So I was the guy who arrested him. I didn't remember the name but I remember him now.'

'What you arrest him for?'

'There were several charges. Passing himself off as a member of His Majesty's Forces. He was low-grade SS. Selling goods on the black market. Being a member of a compulsory arrest category, to wit Fremde Heere Ost—Gehlen's old original outfit. And living off immoral earnings. A string of charges on using property of HM Forces without authority and for being a first-class creep.'

Rochford smiled wryly. 'By God when you boys prefer charges you really do make a show out of it. Any more on him up to date?'

'Yes. Worked for Gehlen for fifteen years. Radio operator then senior section leader. Finally head of special sabotage section. Was dismissed with reduced pension in 1964. Appealed direct to Director of CIA. Got frosty official answer but indications are that he maintained some sort of liaison with senior CIA agents. Contacts through U.S. Consulate Hamburg and U.S. Embassy Bonn.'

'Any grounds given for his dismissal?'

Mills referred back and read out loud.

'Unexplained shortage in organization funds to an amount approximating one hundred thousand dollars at 1963 values. Failure to comply with "en-skid" reference SC49 slash two.' Looking at Rochford he queried, 'What the hell is an "en-skid"?'

'It's a jargon term for an NSCID—a National Security Council Intelligence Directive. They're top value directions, generally from the president himself.'

'Can you check what this one was about?'

'Sure. No problem.'

'This was what Munsel must have been hinting at when he said I should think about Fremde Heere Ost. Gehlen based his recruitment at the start almost entirely on ex-FHO staff, and Lerner was one of them. But he was so low down the ladder that I'd never have thought of him.'

'That was a very good buy, David, that rose for the girl.'

'We'd have found a lead somewhere but this saves a lot of time. I'll clear with McHugh and we'll head for Hamburg tomorrow.'

Mills stood at the window and now the sun was coming up. The sky was layered with pink and there were a few long-distance trucks crossing the Kennedy Bridge over the Rhine. The river itself was turgid and cold grey. It was almost five o'clock.

As his eyes closed and sleep pressed back his head there was a jerky disjointed film behind his eyes. Munsel walking up a sloping field looking very young. Pale blue veins in a close-up of a young girl's breasts. A hand-written envelope pinned to an apartment door. A room in a hospital with a sickeningly sloping floor and cards with names typed on them that faded as he tried to read them. And then a small rectangle of pale brown linen like an old-fashioned sampler with the word 'nymphomaniac' jerkily stitched in pale blue silk, as if by a child at school. There was something he kept trying to remember that was important. Something out of the message from Munsel.

Chapter 11

The late afternoon sun caught the gilding on the massive clock face on Saint Michael's Church. The grey stone seemed almost blue from the cloudless sky, and the three-masted schooner on its fat little globe looked as if it were made from soft yellow gold. The man stood on the dusty grass by the Bismarck Memorial and watched the early commuters as they roared westwards from Hamburg to Blankenese and Rissen. Some of them could have taken the coast road alongside the Elbe, but the fast road saved them at least ten minutes.

There was half an hour to go before he was due, and he didn't know Hamburg all that well. Across to his left was the Millerntor skyscraper, St Pauli's tallest building. That's what they'd told him to look for. He walked slowly up Cuxhaven Allee and then he saw the sign. Everybody's heard of the Reeperbahn, and he turned left and strolled past the strip clubs and porn shops. They seemed to be doing good business and groups of men, with a sprinkling of women, looked silently at the displays in the small windows. As he approached the intersection at Davidstrasse he stopped and looked at his watch again. Five minutes more.

He threaded his way past the dingy faces and hotel to Hans-Albert Platz. A group of drunken sailors were shouting and struggling with police from the nearby station, and he hurried across the road to avoid them. A girl in an old car pulled up beside him and shouted an invitation. She was young and pretty except for a patch of violent purple around her eye. When he didn't respond she'd pulled back her skirt and opened her legs. A drunk on the other side of the car had taken her attention and he'd escaped. He stumbled through corridors of stinking fish-boxes and then he saw it. White letters on a red board said 'Hotel Helga' and a cardboard notice said 'Zimmer zu vermieten'. He left the bright light of the street and walked carefully as his eyes became accustomed to the gloom inside. A fair-haired young man leaned on the reception counter studying the pages of a girlie magazine. He looked up briefly as the man approached him.

'You want a room?'

'I want to see Herr Tiebert.'

The young man slowly stood up, and he looked at the man's face carefully, as if it should be remembered.

'Who's Herr Tiebert, mister?'

'Herr Tiebert is the Postmaster.'

The youth pulled up a flap in the counter, and wiping his big red hands on his apron he beckoned the man to follow him. They went up a flight of stairs and down a long corridor. At the last door the youth knocked and took out a bunch of keys. There was a faint shout from inside and the young man turned a key in the lock, signalled to the visitor to wait, and the door closed behind him as he went into the room. It was several minutes before the door opened again. The youth held it open and beckoned him inside. As he walked in he heard the key turn in the door behind him.

It was a larger room than he had expected. The furniture was modern, of leather and teak, and one wall was lined with books. A man in a silk dressing gown stood in the middle of the room. His sparse hair was unbrushed and he looked as if he had only just been roused from sleep. He was smoking a cigar, and with his eyes screwed up from the blue smoke he was looking at his visitor. He was overweight and he stood with his feet astride as if to maintain his balance. He was almost completely bald and his face was pale and fleshy.

'Who do you want my friend?'

'Herr Tiebert.'

'And who is he?'

'Herr Tiebert is the Postmaster.'

The big man rocked gently on his spread feet and nodded as if in agreement with what had been said.

'And who are you?'

'I've brought the American collection.'

'Where is it?'

The man thrust forward a heavy parcel wrapped in crumpled brown paper and tied with thick sisal cord. But the big man half-smiled and shook his head.

'You open it, my friend.'

When the knots were untied and the paper removed there was a thick book with brown covers. Half-calf and buckram, with gold embossing. Right in the centre was a gold circle enclosing a representation of the United States eagle.

The big man took the book and shuffled to the wide desk, and as he sat down he waved towards the leather couch, and the messenger moved over and sat down. At the desk each page was carefully turned and examined. After a few pages the big man opened a drawer and took out a jeweller's magnifying glass and held it to his right eye.

He looked for a long time at the first page. There were two stamps, each in a cellophane cover, mounted side by side in the centre of the page. They looked exactly the same, a circle of asterisks, and inside the circle were the words 'Alexandria Post Office. Paid 5'. There were no perforations. His lips moved slowly as he counted the asterisks. The one on the left had 39, the one on the right 40. He swivelled his chair and took two books from the shelves behind him, as he lay them on the desk he opened one of the drawers and took out a small electronic calculator. The red covered book was Scott's catalogue of the postage stamps of the United States, the smaller book was the German Michel Katalog. For ten minutes he turned the pages of the album and compared references in the two catalogues, and tapped the keys of the calculator gently with the blunt end of a pencil. When he had finished the figures that glowed in red on the small screen were 594,700.00. He tapped three keys slowly and precisely and the calculator converted the figure from US dollars to Deutschmarks. He did a quick sum in his head and then looked across at the messenger.

'Your percentage is five thousand, nine hundred and forty-seven dollars.'

The man shifted uneasily as he spoke.

'I'd been told it would be seven thousand, Herr Tiebert.'

Tiebert nodded his head as the man spoke.

'They hadn't allowed for two things. First is that I have to sell quickly. The second is that it's a small market in Europe for United States stamps. I'm not saying it's not a strong market, mind you. Just that it involves a small number of people. They meet, they talk; I've got to be careful.'

'That is surely between you and the people in Washington.'

Tiebert sucked his teeth slowly and leaned his great bulk back in his chair as he looked at the man in front of him. Tiebert had been told about the little man. He didn't give a damn about the difference of a thousand dollars. He just had a natural instinct for wheeling and dealing.

'They paid your fare, Mr . . . er . . . ?'

'Mr Cosgrave. Yes, they paid my fare but not my expenses over here.'

'How long are you staying, Mr Cosgrave?'

'Well, tonight of course, and I'd thought maybe one more night.'

Tiebert nodded sympathetically.

'Of course. No good coming to Hamburg and not seeing the sights.'

He watched Cosgrave's face, just keeping back a smile

as he saw embarrassment conflicting with a basic interest.

'They did say, Herr Tiebert, that you could maybe help me there. The sights, I mean.'

Tiebert smiled and leaned forward with his arms on the desk. He was used to men like this and he knew how to deal with them.

'You want a girl, eh? A nice young girl?'

Cosgrave looked at the fat friendly face. No longer was it hostile or indifferent.

'Well, that's what they mentioned.'

Tiebert turned back to the shelf and pulled out a bound album and opened it briefly to check, then snapped it to and pushed it across his desk.

'You choose one, Cosgrave.'

As Cosgrave leafed slowly through the pages Tiebert fumbled in his dressing gown pocket for matches and lit another cigar. He waited patiently. Almost five minutes later Cosgrave passed the album back with the pages open. The left-hand page was blank but on the right-hand page were three photographs of a girl and typewritten notes about her statistics and capabilities. Tiebert glanced at the page and nodded his seeming approval.

'Very good taste, Mr Cosgrave. That's young Lili. A very smart girl. Now how about we raise the money to six thousand two fifty. You stay here for two nights. I provide young Lili and half the return fair. That OK by you?'

'The girl stays with me all the time?'

'Certainly. And next month we can make a similar deal. Any girl you fancy in the book. Your choice.'

'I'd rather you paid all the fare, Herr Tiebert.'

Tiebert looked serious, as if Cosgrave had gone too far.

'You speak German, Mr Cosgrave?'

'Pretty well. Not bi-lingual.'

'Yes. It just struck me that Lili only speaks German.'

'That wouldn't be a problem, Herr Tiebert.'

Tiebert reached for the phone and pulled it towards him. He dialled twice and waited. As he waited he looked up from the phone and nodded.

'We'll pay the whole fare.'

Cosgrave smiled his pleasure.

'Who's that? Ah, Heinz. Tell Lili I want her up here right away. No, no ticket. She'll be occupied till Thursday midday. Right. And tell Rudi I want an economy-class ticket to New York on the afternoon flight on Thursday with pre-paid transfer to Washington. That's it. Name? Oh, Cosgrave. US citizen travelling on business. OK.'

And he hung up.

'They tell me you'll be doing this trip every month now.'

Cosgrave nodded but his mind was elsewhere. Then the key turned in the lock and the door opened. The girl was nineteen but she looked about seventeen. The blonde hair was fashionably short and unwaved. She was prettier than in the photograph and as both men looked at her she stood at the door letting them look. She wore a lacy black bra and a thin black suspender belt with long straps to her stockings. Otherwise she was quite naked. Then Tiebert spoke to her strangely gently.

'Lili dear, this is a great friend of mine. He'll be staying with us for two nights. I want you to look after him. Keep him happy. You fix all the meals and so on. Take the Goethe Room, and tell Heinz I want you to have a colour TV. OK?'

The girl smiled and nodded, and with Cosgrave's eyes still on the long shapely legs she stood for a moment letting him look. Then she held out her hand laughing. 'Komm' Du. Wir haben Zeit genug für alles.'

As they left the room Tiebert had reached for the phone again and dialled an outside number.

'Is that you Erich? Much better, thank you. Good news. He's been. Yes . . . yes . . . a hundred per cent OK. We'll make over half a million net. How're you fixed for tonight? Oh . . . to suit you. Say nine o'clock. OK.

I'll contact Fellows myself. About three hours I would think. I'll fix with the girls for when the meeting's over. I know . . . yeah . . . but Fellows expects it. Keeps him happy and saves him getting into mischief somewhere else. OK. See you.'

Chapter 12

Fellows liked only sweet wine and Tiebert had laid on a mass of bottles. Half a dozen were already on the table. He wanted to keep the peace at all costs. Erich Lemke had picked Tiebert as paymaster and administrator because he seemed to have a way with the Americans. They were efficient and tough and they made quick decisions but most of them seemed overeager to get at the girls and the booze. Fellows particularly. But Tiebert's place kept them happy and it was wonderful cover. There was a steady flow of male visitors of all nationalities, for Tiebert's hotel housed some of the prettiest girls in Hamburg. Drunks and toughs were filtered out way down the line. It was discreet, and patronized by important and influential men. The majority were German but there were a few well-informed foreigners.

From the days of the post-war black market Tiebert had been the most successful of all operators. Now he was one of the richest men in West Germany. There'd never been even a vague smell of blackmail in any of his operations and there were a thousand opportunities. Whether it was cameras, watches, girls or coffee that you wanted, Herr Tiebert could supply them. Drugs and diamonds he didn't touch. He reckoned that sort of thing was un-German. He wasn't even tempted, but he'd had plenty of offers.

The American had arrived first and he had opened the safe and shown him the stamps. He'd not been all that interested. As long as they were convertible to hard cash that was all that mattered.

'D'you think you could persuade your people to send over German stamps from now on? These are very special and it's a very narrow market.'

The American shrugged, hands in pockets.

'I can't see why they don't just send over cash.'

Tiebert sighed but explained once again.

'Johnny, we could have used cash up to a year ago. We'd have had a better than four-to-one chance of getting it through. But the whole economic scene is so tough now. All sorts of people want to smuggle money, and all sorts of people want to stop them. The money security is very tight now. Apart from that, if we were caught it's not just smuggling money, it's the danger of the inquiries at both ends. Where did it come from, where's it going. No. It's far too dangerous.'

'You want me to tell them to make it German stamps then.'

'That's it, dear boy. For these wonderful American stamps I've got two, maybe three hundred buyers. For German stuff hundreds of thousands of collectors are in the market. See what you can do, eh?'

Johnny Fellows sat himself down and swung his feet up on to the table. He grinned up at the big German.

'You got that Ruski girl here tonight, Max? Annie, or whatever you call her.'

'Ah, you mean Anastasia. The brunette.'

'That's the one. She's got the best pair of boobs I ever did see.'

'And I guess you've seen plenty, Johnny.'

The American reached for the glass of wine that Tiebert had poured. He sniffed it and drank it down relentlessly. He banged the glass down again on the table.

'You betcha, Maxie boy. That's my speciality—boobs, bottoms and booze. Where's Erich got to? He's late. Nearly twenty after nine.'

Fellows was a big athletically built man, handsome in a rugged sort of way. Tiebert looked across at him with tolerance. This American had proved himself capable and tough, and Erich Lemke had told him that Fellows had brought CIA skills and experience that had doubled or trebled the effectiveness of the operation. Some men, perhaps most men, would have despised the juvenile indulgence in girls and drink. But not Tiebert. He'd made a fortune catering for men's lust and he knew to his profit that most men were much like Fellows but they weren't so open.

The door opened and it was Lemke. He was tall and thin. Elegant and assured. He spoke with a smooth, slightly affected Hanover accent. Nearly sixty now, his career had been spectacular right back from the FHO days. He'd married a wealthy Viennese girl. Despite the aristocratic background he'd met her when she'd been singing at the Palladium in Düsseldorf. Her face was beautiful but Erich Lemke always swore that it was the slender neck and the smooth shoulders that had first captured him. He had never been a Nazi. Or to be precise he had never joined the Party or any of its organizations. With fluent Russian he'd been transferred from the Army to the FHO. Some said that his success against the Russians had stemmed from his love of hunting. His determination and concentration, his uncanny analyses of what the other side would do, were a priceless asset to Gehlen. But when the quarry were captured Lemke's interest was gone. Someone once said he was like a cunning angler, and when he'd caught his fish he would have preferred to throw them back again. Very few people had known of his connections with the CIA and Gehlen. He had been ostensibly head of an import-export company that was one of the organization's fronts. It was the only 'front' that actually made a profit in its own right.

With his wife, he led a high-society life, and was welcome in the worlds of music and the arts, as much as at the Chamber of Commerce. Diplomats sought him out for his views on current events, not knowing that the dialogue would be used as a basis for uncannily accurate reports to others on current international manoeuvring. He smiled at the two of them.

'Aha. I'm last again. My apologies to you both.' He grinned at Tiebert. 'Your friend and client at the Senate waylaid me. The United States' Ambassador has established with the Foreign Minister his country's concern that we are no longer discussing ''détente'' with our distinguished friends in East Berlin.' He smiled. 'He was reassured that it was only a matter of time. Letting the dust settle after Guillaume and all that. He went off happy.'

He settled himself on the big couch and poured himself a drink. The wine was tepid and he made a face and put back the glass, raising his eyebrows at Tiebert. Getting no response he shrugged and turned to Fellows.

'What's new, Johnny?'

'The operation in Warsaw goes live in ten days. Everything and everyone's in place. They've trained so well they could do it in their sleep. They're good boys. Great material.'

'And what about the final targets, what did you choose?'

'The motor-works. There's been a lot of friction there already. Moscow is pressing for price reductions and has slowed the take-off by a third. Everybody'll be sure that it's the KGB putting a spanner in the works. The second target is the security police prison at Cracow. They've got a KGB defector in there. He's been spilling the beans about two KGB 'apparats' in Poland that they didn't know about. When that place goes up they'll be sure it's the Russians teaching everyone a lesson.'

Lemke nodded his approval slowly as he twisted a cigarette into a long holder.

'Have either of you heard any talk about the White House doing a check on the CIA? Or anything in that area?'

The question was aimed at Fellows, who looked surprised.

'Not a word, Erich. Maybe I wouldn't hear anyway. But it's highly unlikely.'

'Not so my friend. An accounting team has moved into CIA HQ at Langley, and is calling in all financial records over the last eight months.'

'That's maybe some left-over Watergate business.'

'Could be. But it isn't. The third set of records they called for was West Germany. And they want everything. Right down to local imprest accounts.'

'D'you know what records they asked for before West Germany?'

Lemke was lighting his cigarette, and he stopped with the gold lighter in mid-air.

'Exactly what I asked, Johnny. The first was Athens and the second was Santiago.' He leaned back comfortably, interested in the American's reaction.

'That's pretty cute, Erich. If they wanted to check West Germany they'd certainly call for something else first as a cover. Athens is legitimate because of their NATO pull-out. Santiago is legitimate because of Allende and the Foreign Affairs sub-committee. But those are both current high-pressure trouble spots. Known and acknowledged. But West Germany isn't in that category.' He paused. 'I'm inclined to think there's something in it. I'll put out a feeler or two. I don't like that one.'

'That's not all, Johnny.'

'What else is there?'

'Ever heard of an American named Rochford? Pierce Rochford the Third to be precise?'

'Yes. But he's not been in CIA for years. Not since after Suez or thereabouts.'

Lemke tapped off the ash precisely into the crystal ash-tray. He reached into his jacket pocket and pulled out two sheets of paper. He glanced at them for a moment.

'Pierce Rochford the Third contacted an old friend of his at "The Farm" eight days ago. Was interested in the current programme. The next day he flew over the area with General Lennox. Rochford was piloting his own plane. Had filed a flight plan that would miss Williamsburg by ten miles. Claimed instrument error for being off course. It was reported to our people at Langley who put a tail on him. He's been in contact with SIS in London. Stayed at one of the safe houses. Flew to Bonn in the company of an Englishman, David Mills. Left Bonn today heading north. Has stopped over tonight at Hildesheim and visited SIS HQ in Hanover.'

Tiebert looked pale and anxious as he spoke.

'My God, Mills was the name of the man who arrested me up north in 1945. They must know something.'

Fellows shook his head.

'Not necessarily, Max. There could be a dozen reasons for them swanning around Germany. The mere fact that Mills is an Englishman makes it unlikely that it's anything to do with us. If the CIA had even a feeling in their bones, they wouldn't be using an Englishman. What the hell's it got to do with London?'

Lemke chipped in quickly. He could see Tiebert's assurance fading visibly.

'I think you're right, Johnny. But I think we'll bring forward the big job.'

The other two nodded and Lemke carried on.

'How soon can you assemble that team, Johnny?'

Fellows shrugged. 'I can assemble them in two days. They don't need training but they need to familiarize themselves with the planning. That could take several days. Even a week.'

'We'll have a planning meeting tomorrow. Nine o'clock suit you both?'

They nodded and Lemke let himself out. Tiebert recognized that it was time to raise the troops' morale and he lifted the phone.

'Heinz, send in some Scotch. A couple of bottles. What? No, we've got plenty. Tell Anastasia to bring it in, and send Magda in too. And Heinz, phone my home and tell Ushi I'll be late. Tell her my love. You know the kind of thing to say.'

Max Tiebert rather liked sex with an audience. Not always, just now and again. With eighteen of the prettiest girls in Hamburg on his pay-roll sex itself wasn't a problem, but there came a time when even firm young breasts and long shapely legs were no longer stimulating. Not every day, anyway. Especially when you're past fifty and the long legs open too readily. Max Tiebert had traded for nearly thirty years in sex and in that time he'd sampled continuously what he offered. But at over fifty he had a feeling that there must be something a man could do to a pretty girl that he hadn't yet discovered. He'd watched in secret while men worked out their lust with pretty girls. Their excitement was obvious, and their satisfaction showed in his receipts, but he never witnessed that missing variation that might fire him anew. It wasn't that he'd stopped having sex, far from it, but all too frequently he would be hardly aware of what was going on. He would 'come to' with his hands cupping resilient flesh, his body moving between complaisantly spread legs. He'd recognize the pretty smiling face but he couldn't remember how he'd got there. He would pay his small tribute and it would be over, but he couldn't remember any words. Wasn't even sure that there had been any words. And as he shook his head to dispel these thoughts the door opened.

Anastasia was carrying the two whisky bottles and Magda a tray with new glasses. They wore only brief black skirts and Fellows grinned as he watched the dark girl's firm breasts as they bounced and swung on her path to his armchair.

'Hiya,'Stasia.'

'Hiya, Yank. How you doin'?'

'Fine, honey. You going to pour out the booze?'

She grinned as she took out the cork and bent over to pour out the drinks. It was their usual routine and she paused for a few moments as his hands fondled her breasts. She saw Tiebert watching as the American's strong fingers kneaded the firm flesh. She wasn't embarrassed. She didn't give a damn. All the girls knew that Max Tiebert got a kick out of watching some man enjoy their bodies. As she stood patiently bent over she saw Tiebert fondling the other girl. Magda was new, only seventeen and not very experienced. She'd been much in demand but was obviously in awe of the big boss. She was doing things to Tiebert but he was still watching the dark girl as Fellows fondled her. Then the American had laughed and said something. The dark girl had stood up, and facing him she lifted up the short skirt. She was facing Tiebert too, and she saw the lust on his face and smiled at him in open invitation. As she straddled down on the American she knew that whatever Tiebert did with the young blonde he'd want her when the American had gone.

There are thirty-two stamp dealers' shops in Hamburg and SIS had reported on them all. All but three had been classified as 'clean'. Mills and Rochford had looked through the reports on the three but they didn't look likely runners. There were no Lerners connected with them and they were only suspect for being commercially dishonest. Rochford had bought stamps at all three but there was no 'smell' about them that intelligence 'covers' generally emanate to the trained observer.

In Lerner's dossier there was little information on his activities since leaving the Gehlen organization. Mills radioed London to check if they had more details. There was a nil report half an hour later.

'Pierce, do you know who is the CIA agent in Hamburg?'

'No.'

'Can you contact the consul and find out?'

Rochford shook his head.

'Wouldn't be safe, David. I made contact with the ambassador at Bad Godesberg because I know he's excluded by the CIA. In some countries the ambassador is left out in the cold. They hate it because it means that the senior CIA man deals direct with top brass of the host country. Makes the ambassador look stupid. Our guy in West Germany is one of these. That's why I was able to make contact with him.'

'Can he help us on this?'

'No. He wouldn't know. Shall I contact the General?'

'What were your instructions on that?'

'Only if essential.'

'OK. I'll try SIS Hamburg.'

'I should go through London.'

'Why's that?'

Rochford grinned. '*You* can't trust the CIA and *I* don't trust your lot. They don't know that we're not still in Bonn, and they don't know why we're here. Keep 'em in ignorance. A few more requests from us and they'll start doing little sums.'

They'd booked in at a small hotel near the Goose Market and they'd paid extra for the top floor with a balcony. Mills had run the filament aerial out to the balcony and taped it up the wall. London were on permanent stand-by but there was heavy static and the decoded signals sometimes didn't make sense. But the message concerning the Hamburg CIA man was clear enough. His name was John Fowler Fellows and he was holed up in a couple of rooms near the Marine Meteorological Office at the back of the St Pauli landing-stages.

They'd hired a car and taken it in turns to watch the street. They were mainly shabby office buildings with a handful of dingy shops and a small café. It had been Rochford who saw him come back on foot about two in the morning. Coatless and hatless, in shabby clothes, but alert and aware, looking back from time to time to see if he was being followed. Mills had taken over at six and had seen Fellows come out just before eight-thirty. He'd stood in the street looking both ways. Then he'd pushed a hand roughly through his thick hair and walked slowly towards the Reeperbahn.

Mills had covered him from parallel streets and had almost missed him as he turned into the entrance, looking away from the hotel at the lorries unloading ice and fish at one of the cafés. Two pretty girls had come out of the hotel as he stood there. They'd looked at him with the speculative air of girls who were used to weighing-up men. He registered them as high-class prostitutes, but they were obviously not looking for business. They seemed unusually pretty and well-dressed for the rough district.

At 9.30 he'd walked over to the café. He'd had two coffees and the waitress was doling out his change when a big Mercedes pulled up at the hotel, and a tall man with white hair had got out, spoken to the driver, and then turned to enter the hotel lobby. Mills was counting out a tip for the waitress, when he said casually,

'What's a guy with a Merc doing at a hotel like that?'

'Didn't see him. Probably Herr Lemke.'

'Who's he?'

'You're not from Hamburg then.'

'No dear. Just visiting.'

'He's a very big man. Politics and several big companies. Got a lovely wife, she used to be a singer. They've got pots of money.'

'So what's he doing at the Helga.'

'Same as all the others I suppose.' She smiled knowingly and watched his face. It stayed blank and innocent.

'It's a place for call-girls. They say it's the best in Hamburg.'

'Who owns it?'

'Herr Tiebert. He's made a fortune out of it. That and the black-market in the old days. Got a lovely house out at Blankenese.'

Mills walked quickly back to the car and Rochford was waiting. They were back at the café again in ten minutes. They sat in the café and watched the hotel entrance for half an hour, but there was almost no movement. One of the two girls returned, and a youth in an apron stood on the hotel steps for five minutes watching the road.

Mills walked alone to the Reeperbahn, found a telephone kiosk and got the address and telephone number of a Max Tiebert in Blankenese. He went back to the car and took the coast road to Blankenese. It was a large detached house near Schinkels park and he parked the car back near the main road. Surrounding the house was a beech hedge but the gates were open and he could see right up the concrete driveway to the triple garage. Two doors were swung up. On the hard-standing was a white Porsche, and in the other garage was a big yellow Mercedes. In a line, across the entrance to the drive, were seven metal circles with small glass inserts. Mills reckoned he was on some sort of target. Seven photo-electric cells meant that someone was taking security seriously. He walked around the block slowly, and on the third circuit he saw a woman getting into the Porsche. She was in her late forties, as smartly dressed as her plump figure would allow, and despite the sunshine she carried a mink stole which she threw on to the back seat of the car. He moved on and she turned left up to the main Hamburg road.

Mills picked up Rochford from outside the café and headed back to the hotel. In their room he turned to Rochford.

'Pierce this is crazy. We can't call on the CIA for assistance. It looks like McHugh doesn't want us to ask SIS directly. We're not getting anywhere. We need proper radio operators, trained men to do surveillance, and quick access to records.'

'Let's see what we've got before we shout.'

'We've got very little. A tip-off from the Munsel girl that a man I arrested in 1945 is involved. That he lives in Hamburg and is a stamp-dealer. It may be a deliberate red herring, or she may be mistaken. Maybe Munsel was deliberately fed false information. We've connected the top local CIA man to a back-street brothel. So what? We're wasting time.'

'We've got more than that, David. My check in the States indicates a positive conspiracy. We've been in Germany three days. That's all. You had to try Munsel, it was required by London. OK, he wouldn't play, but he gave you a tip through his daughter.'

'We'll be here for months at this rate.'

'OK. OK. Phone McHugh.'

And that's what he'd done. Somehow McHugh's precise Edinburgh accent brought things into proportion.

'And when do you want them?'

'Now.'

'They'll be over tomorrow. A man named Lacy will be in charge. They'll travel separately. Contact Lacy at the airport about two in the afternoon. Meantime I suggest you rent a house and set up a working HQ. Lacy will bring cash. If you have any other problems contact me at once and I'll fix it from here. Did you hear the news about Munsel?'

'No, what's happened?'

'He's resigned.'

'Any reason given?'

'None.'

Chapter 13

By midday they had signed a three-month lease of a house facing the St Pauli landing stages. Sandwiched between two sturdy buildings it had survived since before Germany was an entity. It was furnished in the taste of a Hansa-town merchant. Good solid stuff that a man could see was worth the money for the wood alone. Between the two flat brick walls of its neighbours the top storey gave on to a flat-roofed patio. It was not overlooked, and by the time Mills returned from the airport, Rochford had moved in and rigged up an aerial alongside the fire-escape on one of the walls.

The main room on the top floor was turned into an operations centre. Two of Lacy's men had been sent off to watch the Hotel Helga. The radio operator had made contact with London and the relief operator was decoding the inward traffic.

Mills had picked a room to sleep in and work in, and when he had bathed and shaved he reached for the telephone. It was Munsel himself who answered.

'Munsel speaking.'

'Otto, this is David. I heard a rumour that you had resigned.'

'No rumour, I'm afraid.'

'Was it anything to do with our meeting?'

There was a long pause before Munsel replied.

'Yes, I suppose it was. But not in any way that involves you. You're not to blame if that's what you were thinking.'

'What was it then?'

'Hard to say really. We're always coming to forks in the road and having to decide which is the right one. I came to a fork in my road and I decided that neither road was right. So I got out.'

'What are you going to do now?'

'Oh, I have my pension. We shall survive.'

'You don't feel like helping us now you're not an official.'

'David, I'm tired of it all. Without wanting to give offence it seems like kid's games to me. Cowboys and Indians. Our team against their team. I've had enough of it.'

'It affects a lot of countries. A lot of people.'

'The weather does that. But I know what you mean. When I see the Russians tramping up my garden path I'll do something. Until then I'll ride my horses and grow my roses.'

'Can I keep in touch?'

'My dear David, nothing has altered. You're welcome here any time.'

There was a batch of Polaroid pictures from the surveillance team at the Hotel Helga. Erich Lemke had visited the hotel mid-afternoon and had not left until ten in the evening. Johnny Fellows had paid three visits and was still in the hotel. One of the men had attempted to book a room at the hotel and had been given the brush-off. Another member of the team had photographed Tiebert's house at Blankenese.

The relief team reported that Fellows had left at 3.15 a.m. and had walked back to his own place. He'd been stopped by a patrol just coming out of the Davidstrasse Police Station. He had appeared to show them an identity card and they'd saluted when they handed it back. Tiebert had not been identified but the check on his house indicated that he had not returned there. London had reported that Lerner could not be traced during the previous year but there were further indications, some unspecified, that he maintained a contact with CIA in Hamburg. There was a précis report of a Soviet démarche to the Bonn government requesting immediate action against 'a sabotage team operating against the Warsaw pact countries, using ex-Gehlen men and supported by the CIA and West German revanchists'. An extreme right-wing member of the Bundestag had been reported as saying in public that 'the Reds were threatening to occupy West Berlin'. He had indicated that they were going to be taught a lesson before long.

They'd used ultra high-frequency walkie-talkies to liaise with the watchers at the hotel and Tiebert's house.

Mills studied the photographs of Tiebert's house and a large-scale map of the surrounding area. He decided that he needed to look over the house as soon as possible.

It was about one o'clock when he left the car and checked with the watcher. The blonde woman had returned with another woman at 21.15. The other woman left just after 22.00. The lights had gone out at 22.30 except for the inside hall light. That could mean that Tiebert was expected home. But the three garage doors were closed and the big main gate was bolted and padlocked.

By two there was a faint mist from the estuary, and a boat was signalling with her sirens. There was still a faint groan of traffic on the main Hamburg road. He went into the garden from the garage roof of the next house. Standing in the shadow of the hedge he waited to see if there was any reaction from the house. There was none. At the rear of the house the garages projected and joined with a long narrow building divided by partitions to house a laundry unit, a games room and a room with no outside or inside windows. There were narrow white lines across the concrete area to the house. He guessed that they were the dry areas on the concourse where cables were housed. The thin covering layer of concrete over the cables dried quicker when wet than the main area. He threaded through them like some careful hop-scotch player. The security wiring on the rear of the house was tucked under Virginia creeper. He bared an inch of both wires and put the minimeter on the bare copper. They were balanced low voltages. With a probe on each wire the needle swung back to zero. He stripped a piece of wire at both ends and laid it in one movement to both bare sections. There was no spark and no bell. He retook the reading but it was still zero. The wires that went through the thick door frame he snipped and folded away from each other. There was no current in the lock and he laid the strip of double-sided tape on the glass pane nearest the handle. He left four inches of tape on the glass and pulled back the two ends to make a grip. He cut right to the edges of the pane and pulled gently on the tape. He tapped one corner softy with the round end of the glass cutter and the pane came away smoothly and easily. He reached through and turned the knob. It turned easily but the door wouldn't give. There was a bolt at the top. He could just reach the bolt but not well enough to apply leverage to move it. The little battery-operated drill purred and the bit went through the top of the door frame. He pushed home the long metal dowel. There was already a loop in the piano wire and he hooked it over the bolt lever and then looped the wire till it hung on the dowel. He jerked the wire downwards twice and then pulled with the wire over his shoulder. Slowly and evenly, and the bolt moved very slightly. He stuffed in a wad of plasticine where the head of the bolt would strike and pulled again on the wire. The bolt moved forward twice and then came out quickly, the noise of its contact smothered in the plasticine. The door opened easily.

He shone his torch on the floor. It was block parquet and the pattern was even. The dust in the crevices was even all over. On the right was a big sitting room and his torch went over it slowly. Everything was expensive. Teak furniture, fine china and glass, good modern paintings. There was a portrait in oils over the massive stone fireplace. Mills moved over to look at it. It was the blonde woman when she was younger. Say when she was thirty. She reminded Mills of someone, he thought it was maybe some film star. A very blonde one. Jean Harlow perhaps. The big blue eyes and the half smile had a bedroom air about them that wasn't contrived. The girl looked as if she wasn't aware of the sex appeal she exuded. But the nose wasn't Harlow. But it was definitely familiar.

There was a row of silver-framed photographs ranged along the shelf of the fireplace. The first one was a wedding group. Bride and groom smiling at each other on the steps of a municipal building. The bride was the blonde girl from the farmhouse in Glücksburg, and the groom was Scharführer Max Lerner.

Chapter 14

A door in the far wall was closed and locked, and it took twenty minutes testing for security devices, but it was 'clean'. It was an expensive rim-lock with a reverse double-action on notched tumblers and an angled ward. It kept him busy for six minutes.

The room was quite small with two leather armchairs and a swivel chair at a wide oak desk. Above the desk was an oil painting, a street scene showing old houses in Pöseldorf on the outer Alster, Hamburg's Chelsea. Mills gently touched the frame but it didn't move. He gripped it with both hands and as he pulled, it had folded open on hinges set in the wall. Behind it was a small grey safe with a combination lock. But he had no equipment that would open a solid modern safe. He closed the oil painting back to the wall and stooped to the desk. All the drawers were locked, but they responded easily to the skeleton keys. But there were four different locks. In the three drawers on the left-hand side were red-covered ledgers with the years embossed on their spines. They covered the last ten years. As he turned the pages he saw that they were in some private code but the figures were in millions. In the top drawer on the righthand side were insurance policies in the name of Lerner and the deeds to the house and the Hotel Helga.

In the second drawer was a magnifying glass and six folders with plastic sheets holding negatives and contact sheets. The photographs were 2¼-inch square and on the reverse side of each was the girl's name, a man's name and a date. The dates spanned fourteen months. Below the folders were a dozen stamp-album leaves with cellophane cover sheets. On each sheet there were empty spaces where stamps had been removed. On the first sheet there were six stamps left, they were all deep blue, value 5 cents and across the top were the words 'Signing the compact'. On the second page was a single stamp, the centre was blue and showed an old-fashioned monoplane flying upside down. The frame was a dull red and the value 24 cents. On the other pages were other US postage stamps but there were more empty spaces than stamps. There was a small hard-backed notebook and the first ten pages were filled with names and figures. At the bottom of each page were totals. The figure on the last page was almost a million marks.

In the third drawer was a Luger and a silencer, with cardboard boxes heavy with ammunition. At the bottom were two manilla file covers. In the first was typed correspondence with an outfit called Metro Travel Inc., with an address in Washington. There were at least two full-stops missing in each letter where micro-dots had been lifted off. The second held birth certificates for Lerner and his wife, a marriage certificate, German passports for both of them and separate American and German passports in the name of Max Tiebert, occupation—'Geschäftsführer'.

Back at the new headquarters Mills radioed London with a description of two of the stamps, and asked for an indication of their value. By the time he awoke there was a decoded reply on his message pad.

'Your signal 75 stop Stanley Gibbons valuation as follows stop. Inverted airmail approx 40 thousand pounds sterling repeat 40 thousand pounds sterling stop Signing the compact two fifty pounds sterling repeat two fifty pounds sterling each stop Willing buyer willing seller basis stop Joint Int Bureau 4095/17 ends.'

Rochford was still asleep and he shook him awake.

'Pierce, we've got the first break. Tiebert, the man who owns the hotel, is Lerner. The man I arrested, the man

Munsel tipped us off about. He's the paymaster and he's getting the CIA cash in US postage stamps. Rare ones, really valuable ones.'

The American's glazed eyes closed as he lay back.

'They knocked off Lacy last night.'

For a moment Mills was stunned with shock and the total unexpectedness.

'What happened?'

'He was tailing Fellows from the hotel. Fellows went in a telephone kiosk, made a quick call and came out again. He went up to the Reeperbahn and then turned back down Taubenstrasse. Lacy ought to have rumbled that it was phoney. The Reeperbahn's not on the way to Fellows' pad. Anyway, half way down Taubenstrasse Lacy was jumped by three men in a Volkswagen. They coshed him, bundled him inside and drove off. Our second tail walked right into it. He'd gone the other way and was quartering back up Taubenstrasse. He got the number of the car but we'll never trace it without the police. You'll have to get London to check for us.'

'Fellows must have spotted Lacy and called out the dogs.'

'I told you way back, Fellows is no fool; he's a very experienced operator.'

'I'll signal London right away.'

'Forget it, David. They won't risk giving the game away by contacting the police.'

Mills sent off the signal but with no great hope. There seemed nothing they could do for Lacy without a lead. He detailed an extra tail on Fellows.

Pierce Rochford was shaving when Mills went into his room, and the American spoke without turning his head.

'How d'you get on at Tiebert's house last night? He never left the hotel by the way.'

Mills told him about what he had found. Rochford sat on the toilet seat half his face still covered with foam. He wagged his razor to emphasize his words.

'I did a bit of checking last night.'

'On what?'

'Not on what. On who, or is it whom?

Mills didn't answer, he stood hands on hips, irritated and slightly aggressive. Rochford recognized the signs and was faintly amused. He smiled as he spoke.

'I've found out where Larry Polanski's holed up. That's where the action's at, not at the Hotel Helga. That's just admin. There's a real band of boy scouts with Polanski. Full of discipline, it's all military. Guards, patrols, lookouts, forward check-points down the street. Like a marine boot camp on Commandant's inspection.'

'Where are they?'

'Bang outside Hamburg City Hall. Well, nearly. They've got two adjoining apartments in a luxury block in Rathausstrasse. First floor up. You can smell ozone from the transmitters at the bottom of the stairs. The whole of the first floor is theirs. A goon on each staircase and the lift doors padlocked. They're up to something, David, and it's going to be soon. They couldn't go on like that for long without getting spotted. It's like an occupation army.'

'How'd you pick up Polanski?'

'I did the rounds of all the hotel bars near the Inner Alster up to Lombardsbrücke. I hadn't got Polanski in mind particularly, but CIA top brass like the four-star places. Our Larry was in the bar of the Atlantic. He was doing a fast line with a broad and he was too busy eyeing her cleavage to notice me. I was behind him, and I backed out and waited. I've put two men on it. OK?'

'That's fine. We're beginning to hear the music. Marvellous.'

Mills looked cheerful again. They had been wandering around in Limbo for too long.

He went up to the operations room and checked through the messages from the watchers at the Blankenese house and the Hotel Helga. At the house everything was normal. Two women visitors and a cleaning lady had gone to the house between nine and ten and were still there. Most of the visitors to the hotel had not been identified, but photographs had been taken in most cases. Rochford came in and started to read through the pile of paper.

'What do your people use for modern combination locks?'

Rochford looked up. 'You thinking of the safe at Tiebert's house?'

'Yes. I'm thinking of going in again tonight.

Rochford shook his head. 'That would be crazy. They can't help but notice how last night's entry was done. They'll know it wasn't a casual thief. Forget it, David.'

'What *do* your people use?'

Rochford half smiled 'Your people still use a cone over the lock don't they? An X-ray cone.'

'Yes, but we'd need to send for one.'

'Takes a minimum of twenty minutes for it to register.' He smiled across at Mills. 'Our boys can do that now without a cone, without any contact at all. We can do it remotely. Up to a hundred and fifty metres and in daylight or dark. A little gizmo that NASA and Kodak dreamed up.'

'How long to get one from the States?'

'You've got three in London on trial. McHugh could lay hands on one and send it across by plane. You could have it by this evening. It's not radio-active like the cone.'

They picked it up at the airport at four that afternoon. It looked like a 35-mm reflex camera with no lens and a hump on top.

When Mills got back to the house there were two signals from London. They'd pulled their fingers out. There was the address of the registered owner of the Volkswagen. The second signal was brief. It asked him to contact Munsel quickly.

Munsel's voice was tired and deflated.

'Thank you for calling, David. I've got a problem. I need your help.'

'What's it all about.'

'It's Jutta. She overhead me speaking to you. She knows

you are in Hamburg and has gone up there to find you. Thinks she can help you. You seem to have impressed her a lot.' He ended lamely.

'D'you know where she is?'

'Yes, I did a bit of checking, she's at the Vier Jahreszeiten. Nothing but the best for that girl.'

'What would you like me to do, Otto. Send her back?'

'Maybe you could talk to her—gently. Her mother and I are very worried about her.' And there was a catch in his voice as he finished speaking.

'I'll try and contact her tonight. I'll keep in touch. Don't worry.'

'Thanks, David.' And he hung up quickly.

He left a message for Rochford that he had gone to the girl's hotel.

The Vier Jahreszeiten isn't the biggest hotel in Hamburg, as Claridge's isn't the biggest in London. But they've both got world reputations for slightly old-fashioned luxury. The kind of places that the old rich go to rather than the new rich. He asked at reception for the girl's room number and the clerk looked at him knowingly. The message seemed to have got around already. She was in and the clerk pointed to a house phone. It was a languid sexy voice that answered but he heard her catch her breath when he spoke. She was on the fourth floor and she was waiting outside the lift when it stopped. She looked beautiful. There was no use pretending. There was a kind of golden aura, a vitality that could not be denied. She was wearing a woollen dress, cream with brown and caramel stripes. He'd guess Courrèges, but it could just as well be Kaufhaus. An elderly couple left the lift with him and they were startled as she threw her arms round him and put her mouth up to be kissed.

'How did you know I was here, David?'

'Your father telephoned. He's very worried.'

'How on earth did he know I was here?'

'He knew all right.'

'I know. He'll have used his influence. Probably got the police Chief to check for him. I think he knows him. Anyway you're here.' And she linked her arm in his and walked him down the corridor to her room. He sat on the big bergère couch, and she said, 'Let me get you a drink first. Then talk to me.'

'I'll have a whisky then—nothing in it. No water, no soda, just whisky.'

She poured it out carefully and then poured a coke and sat beside him. Her pleasure shone out, and despite his intentions he was flattered and his smile was real.

'I gather you've come to rescue me.'

'Well, help you more. I know lots of people in Hamburg. I don't know what it's all about but I do want to help.'

'Jutta, you're a honey but you mustn't get mixed up in this. And apart from that your parents are genuinely worried. They're not pretending.'

She wrinkled her nose and shook her head.

'It's too late for that, David. It really is. I'm a woman, not a girl any more.'

He laughed, but it was a loving laugh.

'You'll be a wonderful wife before long but right now you *are* a girl. A lovely one, so don't throw it away.'

The big blue eyes were on his face. 'David listen. Men have been after me since I was sixteen.' She shrugged. 'I wish now I'd not gone along with it—the sex bit I mean. I'm not a girl and if I am I'll change for you. I'll prove I'm a woman. I will.'

He reached out and took her hand. 'Jutta, you don't have to prove a thing to me. What about you going home, and then when my business up here is finished I'll come down and see you. We'll get to know one another.'

Her head was bowed. She looked at their twined hands, the whiteness of hers and the brownness of his. To hide her tears she didn't look up.

'I can't wait, David. I need you to care about me now.' She sounded so very young. And defenceless.

He stood up, her hand still in his. 'I'll have to go now. I'll phone or call in later this evening.'

She stood up. 'OK. Let me put on my coat. Which way are you going?'

He smiled. 'To St Pauli. The number is 22-03-41. Scribble it down.'

She smiled. 'No need. I'll remember.'

'Where are you off to?'

She looked faintly embarrassed and turned to look for her bag. 'Just to see some friends I met. They invited me out. I'll call and tell them it's off. I'll come straight back here and wait for you.'

They walked hand in hand along the Jungfernstieg, and the pleasure boats were still cruising on the Alster. It was barely dusk but their lights were on and music came faintly over the water. They waited for the traffic at the City Hall and ten minutes later she pointed to the right. She seemed unusually silent as they walked. Then she stopped outside the entrance to a block of flats and kissed him. 'I'll be back at the hotel inside half an hour. I won't go to bed till you call or come over. However late it is.' Then she pointed. 'Go down to the corner to Johannisstrasse. There's lots of taxis there.' Half way up the steps she stopped, turned and waved to him.

Rochford was waiting or him impatiently. He was wearing headphones plugged into the control receiver for the walkie-talkies. As he lifted them from his ears he looked tense and angry.

'What's going on, David?'

Mills sat down at the table, and because he was ruffled at the American's tone he settled himself elaborately before he looked across at him.

'You tell me, Pierce. Something biting you?' Rochford's face flushed despite the tan, and his eyes were full of open anger.

'I'll goddam say there is. Read that and tell me what it's all about.'

He shoved the message-pad across the table and a nicotine-stained finger jabbed at the text half way down the page.

'15.25 hrs. Subjects LUTZ and unidentified (believed KENNEDY) returned from direction of St Peter's Church accompanied by blonde girl. Stood talking, conversation inaudible. LUTZ flags down taxi. Girl leaves.

'15.40 hrs. POLANSKI and FELLOWS arrive in taxi accompanied by two girls. One identified as at Hotel Helga.'

Mills looked up at Rochford. 'OK. They're giving the boys some fun.' Rochford's face seemed to drain of its anger. He hesitated for a moment and then lifted his hand from another sheet. Slowly, almost reluctantly, he pushed it across to Mills.

'19.10 hrs. Operation director MILLS approaches on foot from direction of St Peter's Church. Accompanied by blonde girl previously reported with LUTZ and KENNEDY (?) at 15.25 hrs. Girl embraces MILLS and enters apartment block. MILLS goes on foot towards Johannisstrasse.

'19.22 hrs. Party of four enter apartment block. Ground floor residents not concerned this operation. Previously identified.'

Mills' face was drawn and pale as he pushed the report back. He rested his chin on his hand and closed his eyes.

'I'm sorry, David. I guess you didn't realize.'

Mills shook his head.

'My God. What a terrible mess.'

'You'd no idea?'

Mills lifted his head. 'Not the slightest. She hasn't either. It's just a horrible coincidence. I can guess what happened.'

'What?'

'The girl came up because she found out from her father that I was up here. She wanted to help. I said I would see her later or phone her. I'd guess these two picked her up earlier in the day in the bar at the hotel. She's staying at the Vier Jahreszeiten. Just the kind of place they'd try.

Like you finding Polanski at the Atlantic. It'll be sex—nothing more.'

Rochford was silent. Then he spoke quietly and carefully.

'You're quite sure of that, David.'

Mills sighed. 'I can't be sure till I've spoken to her but *I* haven't any doubts.' He looked at his watch. 'It's over an hour ago. She'll be back long ago.'

Reception said her key was still on the hook. He insisted they try her room but there was no reply. His heart seemed to beat very slowly as he hung up. He just looked at Rochford.

'I'd better go back to the hotel and wait for her. Find out what's going on.'

Rochford exhaled smoke slowly to give himself time. 'You've got fond of her, haven't you?'

'I think I have. And I'm sorry for her. She's a mixed-up kid.'

The American spent time tapping every fleck of ash from his cigarette into the tin lid he used for an ash-tray. 'She could find out a lot maybe from those boys if she plays along with them. Maybe she really can help.' And the pale blue eyes were watching Mills carefully.

'Pierce, she's Munsel's daughter. He's asked me to protect her.' He was conscious of the high pitch of his voice.

Rochford nodded without conviction.

'I guess you should go back and wait, David.'

Rochford knew there was no point in speaking against the girl. She was Munsel's daughter and that gave her a flying start. She was the loveliest thing he'd seen for years and that sort of appeal he could well understand. And he'd heard a lot of Mills' background from the records and from McHugh. Mills seemed to be drawn towards female lame ducks. Bearing in mind Mills' background it made faint but crazy sense. The capable, tough operator who was drawn to the weak ones. The drunks and the nymphos.

Mills took the underground at Baumwall to the Rathaus

station and then walked. He felt sick with unhappiness and tense with apprehension. He cared for this girl more than he could bear to acknowledge. He'd like the chance to change her but he realized now that nothing would change her. The pattern was established. And now the promiscuity had become a danger as well as a source of pain. He wished that there was no involvement and he told himself that a few kind words, a red rose and some sympathy weren't involvement. But his heart knew better.

There was music playing as he walked across the foyer and there was the bustle and laughter of elegant people starting a pleasant evening. At the reception desk the clerk checked the key. It was still on the rack. No, it was not possible to hand over the key. Hotel regulations.

He walked towards the lounge and then turned to the stairs. He walked up the thickly carpeted stairs slowly. People coming down saw the tense face and their chattering stopped and they exchanged curious looks.

The long corridor of the fourth floor was silent and empty. There was no joy there this time. Outside her room he tried the knob but the door was locked. He walked down to the end of the corridor to where a fire hose was coiled on its mounting. He felt suddenly hot, or was it cold. He needed to do something. He couldn't just wait. From his wallet he took the thin plastic sheet, and when the lift passed the floor he went back to the door. The plastic bent, then slid in and around the bolt and as he gently pulled it backwards it took the tension and he saw the cylinder rotate as the bolt went back. As he turned the handle the heavy door sighed open. He closed it carefully and switched on the light.

The room was just as they had left it. The empty glasses on the table and the cushions on the bergère couch were still hollow where they had sat together. He walked through to the bedroom. On a table at the side of the bed was a crocodile-skin handbag, big, shiny and genuine. He opened it automatically. There were a few cosmetics, a brush with blonde hair glinting. A ring of keys, a locket and a leather bound diary with a gilt clasp and lock. He looked at the diary and then squeezed the sides together and put his thumbnail along the clasp. It sprang open easily.

There were entries for only the first two months. After that there were sporadic entries of initials and names. There was a page for each day and he read slowly through the scrawl of German script. There were men's names and descriptions of what had happened. It was very, very sick. More like the sex fantasies of a man than a girl. A total awareness of the effect of a pretty face and a beautiful body on a long list of men. Nothing had gone unobserved and unrecorded. He had had such fantasies when he was young. The only difference was that the girl had carried them out. Not always with one man alone. Despite the writing it seemed impossible to connect the descriptions with that youthful golden beauty. There was no hint of love or even affection—just excitement and the list. The names seldom appeared twice and sometimes there was no name, just a description. A waiter, a taxi-driver, a man in a park. He locked the diary and slid it back in the handbag.

On the other side of the bed was a photograph of her parents and a book. He walked round the bed and picked up the book. It was an anthology of Poetry. There were translations of the Shakespeare sonnets and as he turned the pages the book fell open. There was a dry red rose pressed between the pages. The head dark red, almost black, and the stem turned back on itself and brittle. It lay against the Hamlet soliloquy and the first two lines were underlined in pencil: 'Sein oder nicht sein, das ist die Frage . . .' He put down the book, walked to the bedroom door, switched off the light, and stood with his eyes closed for a moment.

Back in the lounge he looked at his watch. It was ten. When the chips were on the table it was clear that he didn't really matter. She hadn't come back to sit patiently for his call. He went over to the light switch. He'd wait in the dark and then she'd have no chance to dissemble. But he turned away and walked over to the couch and sat down. Dissemble what. It was all too nightmarishly obvious. He'd accept the story whatever it was. All he needed to check was her knowledge of what her pick-ups were doing. He felt colder and colder as the time went slowly by. Somewhere across the river a clock struck the quarter and it was after eleven when he heard the footsteps hurrying down the corridor. Almost running. Then the key in the door and she burst in.

She was wearing the pale beige coat and she had some material slung over her arm. Her face was flushed and her hair awry. She made for the telephone and as she sat on the upright chair he saw that under the coat she was naked. The material she had thrown to the floor was the woollen dress. Her out-stretched fingers reached for the dial and her other hand pushed back the long blonde hair and slid back the top of her coat. She was dialling the second number when she suddenly turned and saw him sitting silent and still, watching her. Slowly she put down the receiver. The full lips parted, her eyes big, and a red flush mounted from her neck to her cheeks. She sighed and he was ashamed that he noticed the lift of her breasts. He noticed too the rosy marks where they'd been handled. Her hand went to her forehead for a moment and her head was bent down. Then she smoothed back her hair and turned to look at him.

'David, oh David. What will you think?'

He felt full of anger, angry questions, and the bilious comments of a jealous man. He breathed deeply to control his feelings. His eyes on her face but aware of her naked breasts. His voice came out dry and strained.

'You don't have to make any explanations to me, Jutta. Just answer me two questions.'

'Ask me the questions.'

'Did you know who the men were before you went there?'

'I knew their forenames. Hans and Mickie. I met them downstairs in the bar. I didn't think I'd find you for days.'

Her face was white and she looked ill. 'I was stupid. Horrible. But I was unhappy. What was the other question, David?'

'Did you know what they were up to when you went back this evening?'

She shook her head and her eyes pleaded to be believed. 'I didn't know anything about them. I only went down there to tell them I wouldn't be seeing them again.' She shrugged. 'I was afraid they might turn up and spoil things with us.'

'So why did you stay?'

Her fingers played nervously with a button on her coat and he was sure she was working out some intricate pattern of lies. She looked up at him.

'If I don't tell you the whole truth you won't believe me. But I wish I didn't have to.'

She waited for him to respond, but he sat there silent and grim faced.

'When I got there there were a lot of men and some girls, and Hans and Mickie took me to one of the other rooms. We had to pass through a sort of big office. There were guns on a table and radios. Not ordinary radios but large metal ones. A man shouted at them to take me out of the room, and they took me to a room at the back. I told them I couldn't see them and that I was going straight back to the hotel. They were very excited for me. They said they wanted sex before I could go. I said I couldn't stop, that maybe I'd go back some other time. They were very angry. They said they would not be allowed out for a week and they wanted sex with me.' She paused and then went on. 'I said I would do certain things and let them do certain things but I wouldn't have sex all the way. And I told them who my father is to frighten them.' She hesitated again, then sighed, and her voice was flat. She looked at his face. 'So I undressed and let them look at me and touch me. And I satisfied them. That was all I meant to do. Then Mickie went off and Hans stayed with me.

'He wanted more sex with me and I said again that I'd come another day. He was very eager and said they could not go out for five days and after that they'd be gone. I asked what they were all doing sort of hidden away, and he said I'd read all about it in the papers next week. And then a big fat man came into the room and asked if I was Munsel's daughter. When I said yes he asked me questions about daddy. Silly sort of questions, but he nodded when I answered. And then he asked if an Englishman had been to the house and I said I didn't know, that I wasn't always there. And then he gave a sort of grin and said if I was Munsel's daughter I could pay an old debt and he fetched a camera and a flash thing and took pictures while Hans and Mickie did things to me. Then he went off with Mickie again and Hans stayed with me. I guessed by then that all this was something to do with you. There were things Hans wanted me to do that I wouldn't do. I said I'd do it if he told me why he couldn't see me some other time. He asked me what I was doing in Hamburg and I said I had run away from my parents. All the while he was touching me and asking me to do this thing. Then he was called away. I could hear him and two other men talking in the passage. They were arguing about something they were going to do. And I guessed this was why you were in Hamburg, and maybe why you had been to see my father. When he came back he wanted me to get out quickly. He took me downstairs by a fire-escape, and I came back here to get in touch with you.'

He believed what she had said. There was no way to disbelieve it, but he loathed it all.

'And what did you hear?'

'David, I'll tell you, but tell me first. Do you hate me?'

'No, I don't hate you. I don't pretend I understand, but in a way I do. And I'm sorry about it. Sad about it.'

'Do you forgive it?'

'I'm not in a position to forgive or not forgive. I don't own you, Jutta.'

'You do, David. If only you knew. The first bit was me, the horrible part. But the last part was for you.'

'I understand that. I understand. You'd better tell me what they said.'

'They're going to blow up the City Hall while the State Government is in session. They're going to shoot someone. A foreign visitor. They're going to make it seem like the Russians have done it.'

'When does this happen?'

'They didn't say. It seemed like in a few days' time.'

'And the visitor?'

They didn't say who. They just talked about "the visitor".'

Mills stood up and the girl cried out.

'David, please don't go just now. Comfort me before you go. Say I've helped. Don't leave me alone.' She looked at him and said softly. 'I'd die, David, if you went like this.' And he knew it wasn't a threat, it was a fact. In that crazy mixed-up mind there was love for him all right. But there would be no peace for either of them. He wanted to hate her or her behaviour, but he couldn't.

He walked over to the phone. 'I'll have to make a call.'

'Shall I go to my bedroom so you can talk?'

He shook his head. 'No, it makes no difference.'

The call was misrouted and he dialled again, and there was a quick response.

'Get Rochford.' He waited.

'Pierce?'

'Yep.'

'Those people we spoke about. It's bigger than we thought, and soon. I'll see you in half an hour. When I dialled just now I was misrouted, will you check if we're bugged?'

'Hold on.' He was back in a few seconds. 'No. The meter hasn't moved and the needle trace is flat, no dips at all. Tell me more.'

Mills told him.

'Any idea who the visitor could be?'

'None, but we can easily check. I'll leave it to you. See you soon.'

'How's the girl?'

'Fine.'

'And how're you, fella?'

'Fine too. See you.' And he hung up. He turned to face the girl. She was looking up at his face, searching for a clue to his reaction. The prisoner awaiting sentence. 'You did very well, Jutta, it's going to help us a lot. It will save a lot of lives as well.'

'But it was only luck, David. And not a very nice kind of luck either.'

'That's over and done with. Forget it.'

'And what about you? Will you forget it?'

He opened his mouth to speak. Then stopped for a moment and started again.

'No. I won't forget it. I can't. Not for a long time anyway. But it doesn't make any real difference to us. I do care about you and that hasn't changed.'

'Just care—not more.'

'I *think* it's more than care, Jutta, but my mind won't rest to think about it. There's the job I'm doing. There's the problems around you—your problem. I'm confused—but all through the middle of it I care about you—maybe more than care. But we're not of an age and that's another problem.'

She smiled a faint smile. 'That's no problem for me, David. I love you.'

He looked at his watch. 'It's late. After one o'clock.' Against his will he looked at her breasts. When he looked back at her face the pallor was back.

'Have me, David. Have me now. Wipe it out for us both.'

But he knew it wouldn't wipe it out for him. The room would be full of other men. As he hesitated she spoke again.

'Do you want me like that?'

'I'm a normal man, so you know the answer.'

She slid out of the thin coat and stood up holding out both hands.

'Have me just for my sake then, David.'

He took her hand and she led him to the bedroom. He saw the handbag on the table and remembered the pages of description. She lay on the bed and watched as he undressed. He lay beside her and closed his eyes to blot out the ghastly vortex in his head, whirling with men's names and places. But her mouth was on his and his hands covered the soft full mounds of her breasts. His fingers used and enjoyed the firm young flesh as other men had done. And when his hand moved down to smooth the flat belly she took it and thrust it down between her legs. Holding it tightly against her. When she was on her back and he was in her she smiled up into his face and he hated the smile. Too many others had had that smile. But it didn't stop the waves of his lust as he took her.

When he was done he lay beside her, their heads on the pillow, her hand on his chest. Like all the others he'd enjoyed the young body but he wouldn't be going back to his home like the others, to add it to the list and forget it. He shook his head and leaned up on his elbows, his eyes aware of the rumpled sheets and the long shapely legs. Then inevitably he looked at the blonde thatch between her legs and he saw the blood on the sheet. He sat up and the girl, startled, looked where he was looking. She turned her eyes to his face and they half-closed like a dog expecting to be hit. The soft mouth trembled.

'I'm sorry, David. It isn't very nice is it?'

He looked at her incredulously, frowning. 'Tell me.'

She shrugged. 'I've never done that before. I'd never let them do that.'

He felt a mixture of elation, guilt, and revulsion. He was the first, and the biblical proof was on the sheet. He was now more responsible than the rest, and he loathed the fact that all he could think of was what the others had done. He leaned over and kissed her gently.

'I love you, young girl. So let's stop pretending.'

The big smile beamed, and the sun shone, and because he wasn't used to being happy he immediately thought of the job he had to do.

'Pack your things, honey. You'll have to come back with me. You won't be safe here.'

'Why not?'

'They may be worried that you saw too much and come looking for you. We can't take the risk anyway.'

The girl slept in his bed back at the house. Mills bathed and settled at the desk to read the reports. Rochford came in bleary-eyed in his dressing gown.

'Hi. Better fill me in.'

'They plan to blow up the City Hall while the State Parliament is sitting. That will be about four hundred people if you throw in officials and public as well. And as I told you, they plan to assassinate some important visitor. All this in about three or four days' time.'

Rochford lit a cigarette and inhaled before he spoke. 'Can't be for three days. They don't sit till then. I've checked. Guess who the distinguished visitor is.'

'No idea.'

'Tito. On a state visit. They're crafty bastards. Everyone knows that Moscow's had several tries at Tito for going it alone. Nobody gains except the Russians if he gets knocked off. And on a state visit. You could wave goodbye to any thoughts of East-West "détente" after that. So what do we do now?'

'Tell McHugh to deal direct with the German government?'

Rochford shook his head. 'The Germans wouldn't buy that. Say it came out. Dissident Nazis trying to discredit the Soviets? Not in a million years. Either way they lose. If people do believe them, what sort of counter-intelligence do they come out with? If they don't believe them who'll carry the can? They will. Either way they end up with egg on their faces.

'And what about my lot? Unauthorized games by the

CIA in a NATO country. Forget it. They'd probably knock us off instead. Buddy, the ball's right here. You check out with McHugh that he reads it the same way, and I'll check out with the General. But I'm wasting my time for sure.'

Rochford's reply came back first. It was short and clear: 'Rochford on detachment stop Nix stop You deal fast ends.'

As the time crept on to midday they both waited for London's reply and planned for a negative. They sent a man with a Leica and 10 rolls of black-and-white to the City Hall. They wanted all the photographs of places where explosives could be concealed, that he could get—inside and out. Another of the team went to the Information Office who helpfully explained in detail the procedure for sittings of the State Parliament. They also got a press handout with the details of Tito's visit and his itinerary.

Just after one o'clock Mills was called to the telephone. As the radio operator handed over the earpiece he said, 'For you. Personal.'

'Hello. Yes?'

'David, this is Otto. I think I'd better come up and see you if you've no objection.' His voice was steady and there was a rasp of determination in it.

'What is it, Otto?'

'Did you find Jutta?'

'Yes. I've brought her here. She's still asleep but I can wake her if you want to speak to her.'

'What's happened?'

He hesitated for a moment or two and decided to evade the question.

'I thought she would be safer here.' There was a long silence at the other end, so long that Mills thought they might have been cut off.

'Otto. Are you there?'

'Yes, I'm here. If you don't tell me the truth there must be a very good reason. But I think I ought to know.'

'What is it you want to know?'

'David. About fifteen minutes ago a man brought a parcel here. He didn't wait for an answer. Helga took it in. It was addressed to me. Not as a civilian, but as Colonel Munsel. It was stamped "Streng Geheim". Wartime top-secret, we don't use that classification now. Just for safety I opened it in a bucket of water in case it was explosive. In a way I suppose it was. There were twelve photographs of Jutta. Some with a man, some with two men. I won't describe them, David. They make me sick. They're the kind of things men buy from the shops on the Reeperbahn. There was a note inside. I'll read it to you—it was in English. "To Colonel Munsel, arselicker to the English. She likes it best with two men. Tell the English Jew to go back or we'll break you. He's got twenty-four hours. He leaves by air from Düsseldorf. We shall check. Glücksburg 1945." That's all it says.'

'She was forced to do it, Otto.'

'I know my daughter, my friend. She thinks I don't. There is no indication of force in these pictures. Quite the contrary. I know her kind of life and there is nothing I can do. It's far too late. She stands no chance of a normal life now.'

Mills closed his eyes because he knew what he was going to say. He doubted the wisdom but he didn't doubt the fact.

'I'm going to marry her if she wants me, Otto.'

There was a long silence before Munsel spoke.

'Good God, David, you can't know what you are taking on. She's my daughter but I must say it. Your life will be a misery. A torment of jealousy. She won't mean it, or wish it, but that is the outcome. Soon, not late.'

'You may be right, Otto, but that's what I intend.'

'Then I can only say you have our blessing—mine and Helga's. This alters my position. I'd better come up at once. There are many ways I can help you. Tell me where you are. I'll fly up.'

* * *

He went in and woke the girl.

'I've just been speaking to your father. I've told him we shall be married when this is over.'

She was sitting up in bed. Her knees bent up and her slim arms clasped round them. She looked at him for a moment then put her head down and sobbed. He stroked the long golden hair as he spoke to her.

'I need your consent, of course.' She looked up and saw his smile. She said softly.

'You know you have that. I promise I'll change, David. I'll never let you down.'

He looked at her gently.

'It may not be possible, my love. It's not that easy. But either way I'll love you.'

She held his hand in hers.

'They sent the photographs to your father.'

'What photographs?'

'Yesterday.'

'Oh God, what scum. What did he say?'

'He understands, honey. It'll all be all right.' He stood up. 'But until this is all over you won't see much of me. You don't go out. You stay here. You don't answer the phone or speak on it. Your old man will be around. He's helping us.'

The signal from McHugh had come in. It was equally terse and equally negative.

'Your 071105 stop Imperative you deal stop Joint Int Bureau 504 ends.'

Chapter 15

They decided to put off their planning session until Munsel arrived and that was not until almost three o'clock. He'd walked the last mile and was sure there had been no tail. Mills introduced Rochford, ordered coffee, and they sat around the table. Munsel looked brisk and military and he had to control himself not to appear to be taking over.

'Tell me what you know and I'll fill in where I can.'

'We know that this organization is in Hamburg to blow up the City Hall while the State Parliament is sitting. They also intend to assassinate Tito while he is in Hamburg.

'Max Lerner, the man I arrested when you were with me in Glücksburg, seems to be the paymaster. They are getting around half a million dollars a month. It comes over as rare stamps. Lerner sells them and funds the operation. A renegade section of the CIA is supplying the funds and other help. Lerner operates a call-girl racket in a hotel between here and the Reeperbahn. He goes under the name of Tiebert.' Munsel looked surprised.

'I remember the name Tiebert. He's very influential in Hamburg. And Bonn too. Sorry I interrupted.'

'It was Tiebert who took those photographs.'

Rochford raised his head. 'What photographs?'

Mills looked at him. Staring him down.

'They're not significant, Pierce, I assure you.' Rochford took the hint and Munsel relaxed.

'Pierce has pretty conclusive evidence that part of the CIA are involved. What we don't know is how big this organization is. There are about twelve Germans involved up here. This may be only part of the set-up. The American in charge up here is a man named Polanski. Larry Polanski. Was CIA until recenty. May still be CIA. They are holed up in a set of apartments on Rathausstrasse. Within spitting distance of the City Hall. There's one other influential man we've identified. Erich Lemke.'

Munsel smiled. 'Anything else?'

'To round off we are not able to approach the German government or the BND. They won't want to know. It's our immediate aim to put this operation out of action but there may be more to deal with later.'

Munsel nodded. 'You've learned a lot in a week but I can fill in some background for you. Shall I go on?'

They both nodded.

'The German government is as ham-strung as the Americans are with the CIA. They have a suspicion that there is such an organization. They also know that powerful politicians both here and in the States would give it moral support. If a real operation were mounted against these people it would make no headway. They'd be tipped off to every move. Certainly here, the government could fall. Not openly because of these people. Some other excuse would be found. There are a dozen that could be used.

'In private there are open discussions and there are serious politicians in all parties who welcome such an organization. Willy Brandt's attempts at détente with the Soviets were never popular. People saw them as necessary maybe, but there was no heart in it. You can't carry a major policy against the majority of the people especially if the people are covertly backed by the politicians.

'In this case what is there to complain of? A group of private individuals think the Russians are not to be trusted. Is that surprising? The Americans find that all their real intelligence from the Warsaw Pact countries has dried up since Gehlen went. It is the American's policy too to negotiate détente with the Russians. Why were Kissinger and Nixon in Moscow if not for that? Why the massive trade pact with Moscow if not for that? But they too don't trust the Russians. They get no intelligence out of the Soviets except by satellite, but they get enough information out of Asia and South America to know that the Russians only want peace when it suits them. Let's face it, the Russians spend vast amounts in men and money all over the world. With one single aim. To cause strife and industrial chaos. Not for the socialist dream. Not for paradise on earth. Not to protect the Soviet Union. But for conquest.'

Munsel was stabbing at the table with his fingers and his head was down aggressively. Then he went on again. His voice soft now, and even.

'So why are we here? Why do we want to stop these men?' He looked from one to the other but they stayed silent.

'Because these men are not the government, these men are outside the law. If our government and the American Government, the British and others feel that détente with the Soviets is possible then they must negotiate. It is their right. Their responsibility. That is what they were elected for.

'There are three more points. First, the governments seeking détente operate from a basis of knowledge that the ordinary citizen is not privy to. Secondly, however slim the chance, however unfavourable the odds nobody—nobody—can say that it is one hundred per cent certain that some time the Soviets may not want to live in peace. Maybe today is that day. And thirdly, these men, these scum, these Nazis, they don't care if today *is* the day. Like the Russians they too want chaos, they too want us at each others' throats. Where do you find the extremists? You find them demanding more and more permissiveness, they break the law for good ends they say. There was a good Nazi proverb you should remember, "Der Zweck heiligt die Mittel"—the end justifies the means.' His fist banged the table, 'It was not true then and it's not true now. He lowered his voice again. 'So let us be quite clear that what we must do has no platform of morality. We are not heroes—we are just different thugs, different scum. Our end will not justify our means. But—and it matters—we do not work for disruption. We work for peace. That we know. For me I despise my countrymen who do these things. I am not pleased with my part either.'

The argument was sound and both Mills and Rochford were impressed. But they were faintly embarrassed too. They needed no philosophizing to justify their actions. They had been instructed to do certain things. They saw no reason to question their orders.

Mills spoke first. 'Is there any co-operation we can expect? From the police or the authorities.'

Munsel shook his head vigorously. 'None. More likely obstruction. Nobody in Hamburg would move against Erich Lemke for a start. Forget that kind of help.' The others were silent and Munsel waited patiently and then spoke again.

'There is one more thing these people will do. And it affects you mainly, Mr Rochford.'

'What is that?'

'Were you in CIA in 1961?'

Rochford hesitated for only a moment then he nodded. 'Yep.'

'You remember an "en-skid" SC49 slash two?'

Rochford looked out of the corner of his eye at Mills whose mouth was pursed.

'Maybe, Colonel. Remind me.'

'It was from President Kennedy personally. Not his aides, not his office, not from the Director of the CIA, but from the President. It was a total ban on the circulation of, or reference to, the transcript of Kennedy's meeting with Kruschev in Vienna in 1961. Remember now?'

Rochford gave a glance at Mills' stony face. 'Yes, I remember,' he said.

'What about you, David?'

'I know nothing about it. But I've seen a reference to it. It was one of the reasons given for Lerner's dismissal from the Gehlen organization.'

'On June third 1961, at a private meeting between Kruschev and Kennedy in Vienna, Kruschev told Kennedy that the Soviet Union would go to war unless the Americans gave up West Berlin. SC49 slash two covers the transcript of that conversation.' He paused to let the facts sink home for Mills.

'Can you imagine what the publication of that transcript would do for détente with the Soviets? Or trade pacts for that matter? The Germans would be on edge for a decade. The repercussions are unimaginable.' He waited again.

'And that's what these people intend publishing. I'd guess they plan to do it any day now. That, with the blowing up of Hamburg City Hall and even an attempt on Tito, would make the cold war look like brotherly love.'

'How do you know this, Colonel?'

'It has been talked about in Bonn for a month or more. The word had gone out from people in this group to show they meant business. Some saw it as a threat, something to hold off action against this group. But not for me. I knew they would use it when they were ready. I'd say they are ready now.'

Rochford shifted in his chair.

'Sorry, David. They wouldn't release it. That's why I let it go.' Mills raised his eyebrows but said nothing.

Munsel reached for his battered brief-case and drew out a sheaf of papers. He pushed them across the table to Mills. There were five pages of names and addresses.

'Those are my runners, David. Months ago I went through all the old Gehlen files. There are seventy-nine names there of people I can't account for. The addresses are useless. I've checked them already. Not known. I took that as confirmation. We're an orderly lot us Germans. We don't get lost unless we want to.'

'What do you feel will be the reaction of the rest of these people if we deal with the group here in Hamburg?'

Munsel closed his eyes and his fingers tapped on the table as he thought. Then opening his eyes he said; 'I'd guess they would call it a day. And the government in Bonn would spend a lot of time rooting them out. It's strange really, neither the Americans nor the Germans really like what you're doing, but they'll certainly cash in on it if you succeed.'

Mills opened the door and called for more coffee. Someone handed him a message slip. It said, 'Extract from late-afternoon news bulletin Nord-Deutscher Rundfunk: "The body of a man was recovered this midday from the Sandtorhafen. It is estimated that the body had been in the water for less than three hours. The corpse has been provisionally identified as Hans Albert Richter, aged 31, ex-paratrooper. Last known employment demolition worker with a construction company in Hanover. The police are investigating and would welcome further information.'

Mills pushed it between Munsel and Rochford.

'That was one of the men with the group at the apartment block.'

He said no more. And Munsel pushed the paper away.

'What do we know about them?'

Mills got up from the table.

'I'm going to see Jutta. You fill in what we've got, Pierce.'

Rochford stretched his arms and leaned back in his chair.

'A whisky, Colonel?'

'Thank you.'

As Rochford fetched glasses and bottles Munsel pulled a pad from his case and laid it neatly in front of him. When Rochford had poured the drinks he remained standing, glass in hand.

'You mind if I say something, Colonel?'

Munsel looked up surprised.

'Of course not.'

'You were a Wehrmacht officer and after that you were a senior government official. And on top of all that you're typically German. Order, planning, keeping to the rules and all that. Agreed?'

'More or less.'

'Well in this sort of operation that attitude doesn't work.

If these people got the chance they'd kill us. Without hesitation, and without losing any sleep when they'd done it. In my view we only succeed if we do the same. You ain't going to like all this and I suspect you're going to be a brake on what we have to do.'

'Why do you think this?'

'Your summary of the position. No quarrel from me about the argument or the analysis. First-class. But I don't need it, and Mills doesn't need it. We've been asked, ordered, by people in authority who we respect to do something. We're going to do it. Your motives for helping us are too fancy for me. And I think when the chips are on the table you'll be a hindrance. Your motive isn't real enough. You don't want to pay the entrance fee.'

'And what *is* the entrance fee?'

'Stop being a boy scout. Stop being the Staff Officer. Believe these boys are best dead. And be prepared to do it yourself.'

Munsel looked up at Rochford as he swigged back his whisky.

'And what's your motive, Mr Rochford?'

The American smiled and thought for a moment.

'I want a world fit for cowards to live in. These guys are rocking the boat.'

'My motives are more personal than yours, Mr Rochford. When the chips are on the table as you put it, we'll see who's quicker off the mark.'

Rochford had his drink half way to his mouth and he stopped with a wry smile.

'I'd like to believe that, Colonel. I'd like that very much.'

Munsel opened the flap on an envelope among his papers. He pushed a photograph towards Rochford, who, still holding his drink, looked at it carefully.

'That was delivered to me today, Mr Rochford. As you'll see it's my daughter Jutta. It was taken under some duress by the people at Rathausstrasse, and it was sent to me to frighten me off. So don't worry too much about my motives.'

Rochford put down his empty glass and handed the photograph back to Munsel.

'Has David seen this?'

'No. But he knows about them.'

'Don't show them to him, even if he asks to see them. Don't keep them. Burn them. And I'm sorry I misjudged your attitude.' He moved over to the window and looked out on the river. 'One of our men, a fellow named Lacy, was hi-jacked by three men in a Volkswagen. We've got the number, and London have given us the registered owner's address. Anything you could do to help us there?'

'I should think so. Give me the details.'

Chapter 16

There was a Manet, a Renoir and two van Eycks on the long wall. They had their own individual lights and they emphasized the texture of the hand-blocked wallpaper. The elegance and good taste was not all-embracing, but it was the room of a wealthy man, and the gilded French furniture only pointed up the incongruity of the meeting and its purpose.

Apart from Erich Lemke himself, Polanski, Fellows and Tiebert sat around the oval table. When Lemke had locked the door he walked to the chair at the head of the table. He wore a beautifully laundered pale blue shirt, open at the neck, blue denim slacks and soft leather sandals. Even the grey hair on his chest that sprouted above the neck of his shirt looked properly arranged. He pushed the jade ash-tray to the centre of the table but no one else was smoking.

'I understand there were problems with the detonators, Larry.'

'We've solved them now, Herr Lemke. The markings identified them as Czech and that seemed OK. Then we discovered that they're freely available in France so they wouldn't do. We've got Russian detonators now.'

'Genuine?'

'Absolutely genuine. Most of them from a building site in Leningrad and the rest from Dublin.'

'What about the timing devices?'

'The latest. Made in Kiev and only available to the Red Army, the GRU and the KGB.'

Lemke looked across at Fellows.

'And Lacy?'

Fellows shrugged. 'Nothing. He's been unconscious for eighteen hours. Richter was heavy-handed. Probably my fault. I told him we were in a hurry.'

'Richter use pentathol first?'

'Sure. But he'd had preventive treatment. Part of SIS routine now. He just spouted nursery rhymes and multiplication tables—non-stop. What about the police inquiries?'

Only Lemke's diplomacy hid his contempt.

'I shall deal with all that, Johnny. But what a stupid place to dump the man. Why not ask us before doing it? In a strange town what looks like a safe place is sometimes quite unsafe. And to put a corpse in the river on a rising tide is too stupid for words. You might just as well have delivered him to the police direct. The river police picked him up and their doctor did an immediate autopsy. They now know that he was killed before he went in the water, and they know how.' He pushed a cigarette towards Tiebert. 'And now I've got to persuade them that it was a stupidity over one of the girls at Tiebert's place.' He turned to Tiebert. 'And Max, when you issue tickets to your clients for God's sake collect them when they've finished. The man had two of your tickets *and* a porn photo of one of your girls. In this case I made good use of it, but it's careless even for the sake of your usual clients. The police captain at Davidstrasse is not one of your best friends I might say. Anyway, Johnny, just leave that mess to me.' He showed very plainly that he wasn't interested in their agreement. He took it for granted. When he'd changed the cigarette in the long holder he leaned back. 'So what else is there?'

Polanski sucked his teeth to mark his indifference, and waited to see if any of the others spoke.

'We've got a final rehearsal tomorrow.'

Lemke closed his eyes against the smoke.

'Have you seen the change in itinerary for our distinguished guest?'

'No.'

'I thought not. There are two copies over there, Polanski, pick them up as you go out. You'd better have one Tiebert.'

'Does it alter much?'

'Not as far as we are concerned. You'll need to move one of the walkie-talkie men to Helmannstrasse or part of the middle route will be uncovered. Anything else?'

There was silence.

'Well, I've got something for you to think about. Who sent the photographs to Munsel?'

Tiebert shifted uncomfortably on his chair and crossed his arms on his chest as if he were making himself comfortable. But the defensive move didn't escape Lemke's eye.

'Oh that was just a little private thing, Erich. Levelling up an old score.'

Lemke looked at him for long moments before he spoke.

'That, friend Max, was the biggest mistake so far.'

'You think so?'

Tiebert knew he wasn't really expected to answer.

'Well I've got news for you. I arranged for someone to do a little check on Munsel. To see what his official attitude had been when he was liaison at Bonn with the BND. Then I thought I'd arrange a tactful meeting with him to find out a bit about the Englishman. And what do I find? A package was delivered by hand to Munsel. A package that caused him to leave immediately. His wife does not know when he will be back or where he is. Has your messenger returned yet, Tiebert?'

'No, I said he could have a couple of days' leave. We don't need him here till tomorrow.'

Lemke nodded. But it didn't signify agreement with Tiebert. 'So I go back to my friend at the BND and all those old hens were clucking away. What was the messenger's name, Max? Would it be Heinrich Mercker by any chance? As Tiebert nodded Lemke went on. 'Well Heinrich Mercker must have been under the impression that he was riding his motor-cycle at Nürburgring. He was doing over a hundred and fifty k.p.h. on the road out of Bad Godesberg and the police saw him. He ignored their signal to stop and increased his speed. He's in the hospital now at Bad Godesberg. They haven't been able to check completely but there are nine identified fractures so far. Including both legs. Fortunately he hasn't regained consciousness and they expect him to die no later than tonight. On the other hand, and less fortunately, he had one of your pretty pictures in his wallet. She's very pretty, she's a local girl, and her father is an important man. They hand the matter over to the police, who correctly and sensibly, handed it over to the BND, as it concerns the daughter of a recently resigned senior government liaison officer.' He paused to let his little piece sink in. 'And where, dear Max, do you think Munsel might be?' He paused for only a second as he leaned forward in anger. 'He'll be up here, Tiebert, in Hamburg looking for you. And he has friends in the right places so he'll find you. And when he finds you, dear Max, he finds all of us.' He sank back with his eyes closed as if he were exhausted. Then, still with his eyes shut, he asked, 'I gather that Munsel's daughter had left the hotel when you checked?'

It was Fellows who answered.

'We hadn't found out that Richter had been talking till four o'clock. The girl had checked out round about midnight.'

'There was one more thing I learned from my friend in the BND. He showed me a report from their Division Two. It was a monitoring report. For at least forty-eight hours there has been clandestine radio traffic from Hamburg. They are using ultra high-speed transmissions estimated at a ratio of about three hundred to one. Five minutes actual reduced to one second. Seven frequencies randomly used. Identified as a typical SIS format. Impossible to DF it as transmissions are too short. Nearest identification is that it is in Hamburg, south of a line from Havesterhude to Uhlenhorst. In other words they haven't the slightest idea where it comes from. So you can take it that they are up here, that they are operational, that they are supported from London, and that Munsel will probably give them any help he can. So what do you propose?'

Polanski squared up to the table.

'There is nothing we can alter, Erich. It's a matter of days, and the actual day is out of our hands. Maybe we should move from Rathausstrasse, but that will take time.'

'Tiebert, what do you say?'

'I'm inclined to agree with Larry.'

'And you, Fellows?'

'If we weren't stuck with the date I'd say bring it forward.'

Lemke opened his eyes and leaned forward nodding at Fellows.

'Of course, Johnny, of course. And why are we stuck with the date? Because of our distinguished visitor.' He banged his hand palm downwards on the table. 'If we cut out that part of the operation we can bring the rest forward.' He turned his head quickly, like a lizard with a fly. 'How soon, Larry? How soon can we do the rest?'

Polanski didn't hesitate.

'Midday three days from now.' He looked up at the ceiling and his lips moved as if he were counting. 'Midday on Thursday. There's no sitting that morning. There's a reception at the Atlantic after Tito inspects the motor torpedo-boats at the Navy yards. The sitting begins at two o'clock. It's the budget debate, they've got to start promptly.'

Lemke was still for a few moments, and hunched up in thought he looked like some rapacious bird of prey. A fingernail tapped on his teeth as he sorted out the facts. Then he smiled and nodded. 'Yes. That's what we'll do.' He drew a long breath of relief. 'You're happy with that, Larry?'

'Sure. But we'll have to risk staying where we are. What about the Kennedy thing?'

Lemke was pressing the end of his cigarette holder, making circles in the brown-spotted skin on the back of his hand. He looked up. 'Don't worry, I'll deal with that. I'll deal with that for the day before. That's no problem.'

Munsel pulled one of the telephones across the table and checked a number in his diary. He dialled and waited.

'Karl?'

'Speaking. Who is that?'

'Otto Munsel, Karl. I want some information.'

'Nice to hear from you. What can I do for you?'

'I'm thinking of investing in some real estate and I'd like the names of a couple of good architects.'

'Well, Otto, they come in all shapes and sizes. Some are good at one thing, some at another. Depends what sort of property you had in mind.'

'I'm not really sure. I'd like to talk it over with an expert. It's either a total investment, and I'm thinking of say an apartment block like the Müller-Haus on Rathausstrasse, or being part of a consortium in an office block—a high-rise building like the IBM block.'

'Otto, take my advice, don't get involved in an office block for at least another five years. There's plenty of empty office space now, and there'll be more by the end of the year. Apartments OK. There's always a demand if the economics are right. Now the Müller-Haus was named after the architect. His name's Theo Müller. Never been very exciting, but he's safe. Knows what he's up to. Tell him you're a friend of mine. That'll help. He's in the book. Got a practice in Adolphsplatz. Lives near Holy Trinity. You'll find both in the book.'

'Old or young?

There was a laugh at the other end.

'Young. About the same as us. Nice fellow, you'll like him. How's your dear lady?'

'She's fine, Karl. I was sorry to hear about Renate.'

'These things happen you know. One has to let them go their own way. Any chance of seeing you while you're in Hamburg?'

'In a couple of weeks I'll have settled my business affairs and I'll phone you.'

'Fine. Good to hear from you.'

Theo Müller had not been enthusiastic about a meeting so late in the evening, but he was used to the urgent enthusiasms of developers and investors and agreed to see Munsel at his office in an hour's time.

Munsel had walked to the Bismarck monument and taken a taxi. The summer was beginning to break and there was a nip in the air that belonged more to September than August. Müller was waiting for him in the foyer of the offices, and after they had shaken hands the architect had turned and led the way down the corridor to his suite of rooms.

The conference room was surprisingly modern. The long white table was spread with drawings and sketches, and Müller swept them to one end. He was, in fact, much older than Munsel, and his pale blue eyes were half closed as he blinked against the mild light from the ceiling. He wore an old tweed suit, the trousers baggy at the knees, and over his shoes there were old-fashioned grey spats. Across his waistcoat was a gold chain and a gold fob holding a ruby. He took out an old half-hunter watch from his waistcoat pocket.

'I can give you half an hour, Herr Munsel.'

'That's fine. I'm very grateful.'

'Now you said you were interested in a block like the Müller-Haus in Rathausstrasse. Let's see what I can find.'

He went to a modern chest that held drawings and prints. He pulled out the third drawer and checked drawing numbers against a card index. Then with both hands he pulled out four or five sheets and carried them to the table.

'Here we are now. Now this is my original plan. You'll see that the front elevation is very different. I'd allowed for real stone for the cladding. They couldn't afford it in the end, so we changed over to concrete. Kept the general structure much the same.' He pulled out the second sheet.

'Now these are the floor plans.' He pointed with a pair of dividers. 'You'll see that I've met the fire regulations amply, by putting the lifts in the centre and having stairs at both ends. The ducting for the central heating and air-conditioning is enclosed in the walls and floors, and that saves the cubic capacity of four rooms in the block.'

The elderly architect explained carefully the savings and benefits that he had incorporated in his design, and they had gone over original costs and present-day prices. It had not been difficult to persuade Müller to let him study the drawings and specifications for twenty-four hours.

It was after midnight when Mills, Rochford and Munsel started their planning meeting. They had studied the plans of the apartment block and checked with photographs of the building from the street, and from the block of garages at the rear. There were a couple of dozen piles of prints at the end of the table and four manilla folders, each one bulging with papers.

Mills had several foolscap sheets in front of him, and as the other two squared up to the trestle table he started the meeting.

'Over on the left there at the end of the table are photographs that have been taken by the team at the Müller-Haus. Where we think they have been identified there are captions on the back. Where the captions are typed in red it indicates that the subjects are residents of the block and not concerned with this operation. I'd like you both to check these over and, particularly you, Otto, make any comments. As far as I can check there are seventeen men involved in the apartment excluding Tiebert, Lemke, who has never been there, Polanski and Fellows. Apart from four girls who have been regular visitors there are two other men who have visited regularly, and they have been traced to a fishing vessel tied up at the Niederhafen, called the *Torland.* So perhaps you'll both go over that material first.'

Munsel made notes as he checked through the photographs and Rochford smoked and read the captions on the reverse side after glancing at the pictures. After ten minutes they had finished and they moved back to their seats.

'Pierce any comments?'

'A couple. Photograph number four is un-identified. I can give you his name. It's Rex Palmer and he's CIA or maybe ex-CIA, and he's a marksman. Picture number nine is identified as Alf Seenson, that's not quite correct—he's Ralph Swenson. He was definitely removed from the CIA payroll in 1970. Was in charge of a very successful line-crossing network into East Germany. It was operating out of Pullach when Gehlen had his HQ there, and he also controlled a woman agent who was sent to Moscow as a 'sleeper'. She was sent off in 1960 and she was used from '66 onwards. I never knew her name and I can't remember her code-name, but she was high-grade. She was the first to cover the move of KGB headquarters over to the ring-road. She sent extensive details including the new computerized systems. He knows his way around the Soviet operations. That's all from me.'

Mills made notes on the two photographs.

'Thanks, Pierce. Otto?'

'There are four names I can give you of unidentified photographs and I can confirm ten others. Here are the two lists.' And he passed across a sheet of paper.

When Mills had entered the details on the photographs he moved back to his seat. He leaned back and looking at the two others he smiled grimly.

'And now we have to decide what we're going to do. We either tackle them inside the apartment or outside. I'd guess they're not going to be outside very much until they're ready for action. That means inside.'

He waited for the others to speak, and after a few moments of silence Rochford ground out his cigarette and leaned forward.

'We're all dodging the issue, David. And we all know it. You said, do we tackle them inside or outside? What do we mean—tackle? In my book we don't have any choice about *what* we do. We wipe these bastards out. We kill them. In numbers they're two to one, so do we get more help before we start?'

Mills turned to Munsel. He stayed silent and then said, 'Or do we look only at the leaders and dispose of them?'

'They're all capable of carrying on without leaders. They're all top-grade men. Who do we classify as the leaders?' And Rochford looked from one to the other.

Mills was the one who spoke.

'To my mind Lemke and Polanski. I think that Lemke is top man, and he represents the whole of this ex-Gehlen group. And Polanski represents the CIA. A close second.' Mills and Rochford looked at Munsel, who sat silent for a few moments, and then stood up slowly. His chair scraped back as he walked away from the table. He leaned back against the wall, his eyes closed in thought, and his arms folded across his chest. It was a long time before he opened his eyes and his voice was peculiarly subdued as if his mind was on other things.

'Can I suggest that you contact London, David, and ask for reinforcements? Say another ten men. Paratroopers preferably.'

Mills nodded. 'I'll do that. It'll take some time before they reply so let's get some sleep.'

The girl was soundly asleep when Mills went to his room. He eased out a pillow and moved out to a camp-bed in the radio room. The clatter of Morse keys, and the noisy manipulation of tape-recorders, didn't keep him from falling asleep almost immediately.

Chapter 17

Munsel sat in his room and read the report on Lemke from the BND files. He read it again and again. Lemke was a wealthy man, an influential man, he had made few enemies and was independent of any of the political parties. He was an ideal choice to head up this subversive operation but he would have been an ideal choice to lead any group of men where coolness, dynamism and leadership were the criteria. Whether it was a large business or a political party. Munsel read through the summary that he had made, again.

'LEMKE, Erich Maria. Born 24 October 1917. Magdeburg. Father, career officer, Uhlan regiment. On retirement to his estate, invested in agricultural machinery company. Made considerable fortune. Mother, the second daughter of a Prussian Count, Pianist of talent, had been concert standard soloist as amateur. A brother, Georg Adolf, had died aged 14 from tuberculosis.

'Educated at home and Göttingen University. Studied modern languages. Fluent Russian, French and English. Joined clandestine training school for potential officers in 1934. Commissioned in cavalry regiment in 1938. Transferred to General Staff August 1939. Attached HQ Army Group B December 1939. Transferred to Fremde Heere Ost in May 1940. Was arrested Berlin 1945 after the unconditional surrender, with rank of full colonel. Father and mother both killed in fire-raid on Dresden. Released November '45.'

He had settled in Hamburg. Invested in a wide range of

new enterprises one of which was a 'front' for the Gehlen organization supplying travel and transport facilities. This company had been passed back to the control of the Gehlen organization in Pullach in 1964. By then Lemke was one of the wealthiest and most influential men in West Germany. He had married in 1948. She was Maria von Geissburg, aged 20. Born in Linz and educated at one of the Vienna convents. A great beauty whose singing of the old Viennese songs had built her a large following and as many well-paid engagements as she cared to accept. She had continued her career for the first five years of their marriage and then given up her time to the social life that she and her husband so enjoyed. Their large house near Hamburg's Kunsthalle was said to contain almost as many treasures as the Art Gallery itself. They were a popular couple, and their house was always full of international figures from commerce and politics, laced with a number of creative people. Lemke used his influence generously. A word from him had started many promising careers, and a discreet threesome away from the crowd after a lively dinner, had healed many a political wound.

Munsel had met him at several official functions and, typical of the man, he had given Munsel the impression that he had passed some searching test. Where others forgot names and past meetings, Lemke always remembered. He remembered to ask about wives and families. He never implied that he had influence or that he could help. The vivid blue eyes just looked as though they understood every ambition. Even where he made no overt move, he gave the impression that the day would come when some magic word would be said.

People construed his opinions as being in support of this or that, but when comparing notes it often seemed that all he had done was express the case for both sides better than the protagonists had done themselves. A statesman, they reckoned, rather than a politician, and they meant it as a high form of compliment.

The BND reports gave no indication of Lemke being

actively involved in the operations of the Gehlen organization beyond his supervision of one of their companies used to supply routine services to their agents. And all the indications were that Lemke was too big a man in every sense of the word to be involved in day-to-day intelligence work. He wouldn't even have the time.

So why had he been chosen to lead this peculiar team whose individuals, from Tiebert to the Americans, must grate unbearably on his type of personality. And in implying that he was chosen, implied men of sufficient calibre to be in a position to choose such a man. It could not even be said that he was an intense nationalist. He was German in a dozen ways but his lifestyle and outlook were universal, international. His mental eyes always seemed to be on some far distant horizon, far, far from the confines of the Bundesrepublik.

Nevertheless he *had* been chosen, or had chosen himself, and all Munsel's experience and instinct told him that Lemke was the key to stopping the operation.

Mills had wakened early with a sense of doom. Too much unknown, too much to do, and too little time to plan. Only the obvious routes were short enough.

The work done on reconnoitring the City Hall would have to be abandoned. The photographic reconnaissance had shown that there were a thousand places where explosive could be hidden for two or three hours undetected. And if they got that far, it would be too late. They had to be destroyed while they waited. He called in the Royal Engineers' lieutenant.

'Frank, I've got some drawings of a building here. It's the place the other lot are holed up in. We've got to deal with them *en masse.* No escapees, no survivors. I'd like your suggestions.'

Lieutenant Lowe had been seconded to SIS for nearly two years, and he was no longer surprised or shocked by the peculiar uses that his engineering skills were put to. SIS were a law unto themselves, and you didn't ask for reasons, you just responded with your expertise. There need be no inhibitions related to cost or unorthodoxy in the range of solutions. Efficacy was all that mattered. Style and panache were frowned on. The laws of physics and dynamics were his gifts. He remembered the last day of the SIS booby-trap course. For two weeks they had been taught how to bait the traps for others and 'clean' them for their own people. And at the end of that week not a toilet chain, a door handle, an oil-painting or a plastic tile would ever look innocent again. They had been sent, one by one, to the wired-off, derelict village near Bodmin. There would be an extra week's leave for the man who identified the most booby-traps. Lowe had been despondent for he could only register three. The course commander, a thin tough Scot from the Black Watch, had asked each man for his score. When they had all been checked he stood up on an old ammunition box and read out the scores. Some more observant enthusiasts had registered over twenty traps. It had been a cold day, and Lowe remembered the dew-drop on the major's nose. He'd wiped it off with the back of his hand as he leaned forward to talk to them. 'Yui're a bluidy uncouth lot. And frightened as a pack o' wee gairls. I have to tell you, gentlemen, that there's no bluidy traps in the village. You've all got traps on your tiny minds.' He had grinned and stepped down from the box amidst a silence that was markedly unfriendly. Then, as if with an afterthought, he stepped back on the box. 'Oh, by the by, ye've all go' fourteen days' leave. Get your warrants at 'B' company office. Good day to ye, gentlemen.'

Lowe had sat with the drawings for an hour before he called Mills back to the table.

'A lot depends, sir, on aftermath conditions.'

'What the hell's that?'

'Does it matter what happens afterwards. Say, for instance, the building collapsing or being on fire. Other residents being injured or killed. Does it matter if there's a hell of a noise and so on?'

'Ideally nobody should know what's happened for a couple of hours afterwards, there should be no damage to the building and nobody outside that group killed or injured. Shocked, OK, but nothing more.'

Lowe opened his mouth to speak and Mills held up his hand.

'That's the ideal. If it's not possible then we do the next best thing.'

Lowe looked pleased like a schoolboy who had done his homework, and could conjugate the second conjugation's irregular verbs without hesitation.

'What I've got in mind is gas, sir. There's the problem of the number of separate rooms. And there's affected people warning others not yet affected, and there's timing. It would have to be very quick acting or they could be out of the rooms to the rest of the building.

He looked up at Mills for approval.

'Go on.'

'There is such a gas, sir. It's called Charlie fourteen. Kills in less than a second.'

'Why's it called Charlie fourteen?'

Lowe looked startled at such an inconsequential question. What the hell did it matter what it was called.

'That's just a code, sir. I don't know how it's arrived at.'

'Tell me about it. How's it work?'

'It's a nerve gas, kills by inhalation and contact. A few parts per billion are enough if you inhale them, and a single particle in actual contact is enough. It's the second fastest killer we've got. About point four of a second.'

'Why not use the fastest killer?'

Lowe looked uncomfortable. Like a father caught on the hop about the facts of life.

'That's got identifiable after-effects, sir. Rather unpleasant in it's own way.'

'Tell me.'

Lowe shifted uneasily in his seat and then drew a deep breath and plunged in.

'It works on the central nervous system with emphasis on the ear, the balancing mechanism goes haywire and the feed-back from the brain is destructive. The victim is compelled to try to burrow into the ground head first.' He sighed. 'It's very messy, sir.'

'And the gas you recommend. What does that do?'

'It's a sort of instant drowning, sir.'

'For God's sake, what does that mean?'

'The body fluids surge instantly to the lungs. The victim drowns in his own liquids. There's no mess or anything. On autopsy even, the verdict would just be drowning.'

Mills was silent for a few moments.

'How do we get it in there?'

'Ah well, sir. It would take time. About twelve to eighteen hours. Not difficult, but elaborate, and we couldn't take any risks in case they noticed what we were up to.'

'Go on.'

'We pipe to every room leaving about two millimetres short. We pierce those at the last minute. A central feed for simultaneous discharge into all the rooms.'

'What do you need for this?'

'That's the great thing, sir. Nothing special. Plastic pipe, unions, joints, a soldering iron and some clips. The time is taken in the accuracy. Oh, and I'd need a brace and a very long half inch auger—one twenty millimetres would do. And I've got an electronic feeler gauge in my kit. Stops me from drilling too far and coming up in somebody's foot.'

'And where do we do this? Next floor down or up.'

'Have to be next floor down sir. You remember the old law, sir.'

'What's that?'

Lowe blushed for his superior's ignorance.

'You know, sir, volume of gases in inverse ratio and all that. It would rise and come back on us. From down below there'd be no problem.'

'No problem?'

'Well, only for me, sir.'

'What about a gas mask?'

Lowe shook his head and stood up. He knew what he had to do.

' 'Fraid they haven't got around to that yet, sir.'

'Draw money from Parker for whatever you need. But don't buy it around here, go into the centre of town. By the way, how did you reckon we should get the use of the apartments downstairs?'

'Oh the usual way, sir. Wear our gas company uniforms. One copper looking all serious and four gas company men. Urgent checkover necessary. Expenses paid at good hotel—pack bag now—off in five minutes—no mention to anybody—don't want to create unnecessary alarm. I've done it before, sir.'

Mills managed half a grin as Lowe started scaling off the dimensions on the drawings.

Rochford came in wiping lather from his face and holding out a message slip with his other hand. The message said: 'Your 09407 stop Regret impossible meet your request re-inforcements stop Must use present resources stop Joint Int Bureau 1009 ends.'

Rochford smiled. 'Looks like we're on our own. Anything happening?'

Mills told him about the plan he had made with Lowe.

'When are you picking up the gas?'

'Jesus, I forgot about that. McHugh'll have to send it over by RAF plane. I'll send him a signal now. I want it here by tonight.'

'I reckon we ought to have a go at Tiebert. See what's in that safe. Did the CIA gizmo come over?'

'Yes, it came yesterday. Where is Tiebert? Last report I saw he was still at the hotel. Hadn't left it as far as we could see.'

'Yeah, he left once. Was missed by the hotel team but picked up by the boys trailing Polanski. They went to his place at Blankenese this morning at 8.30. His old lady had the police there the day before yesterday. They stayed for a couple of hours. Didn't seem very active.'

'I'll call the team, see what's cooking.'

The team reported that Frau Tiebert had left in the Mercedes. The boot loaded with cases. Had stopped for petrol on the west road and had told the garage attendant that she was going for a few days to Denmark. They didn't follow her from the garage but she took the north-west road that led to Sylt. Twenty minutes later one of the girls from the hotel had been dropped off by a taxi. She had walked round to the back of the house and Tiebert had let her in.

There had been a flurry of signals traffic with London regarding the supply of Charlie 14. McHugh had finally agreed with the proviso that a biochemist should supervise Lowe's part of the operation, with over-riding authority on method of use. The small gas cylinders and the expert, had been flown by jet to a NATO air-strip near Bremen, and Lowe and the chemist had gone into conclave in Lowe's room.

Mills had spent half an hour with Jutta Munsel. Her happiness gave her a golden glow, and she had accepted cheerfully the lack of attention that she would get until the operation was over. She had a short talk with her father and Mills sensed that the tension had lessened between them.

The man who sat opposite Lemke wore a sports coat and tight blue denims. He was not Lemke's idea of a foreign correspondent, nevertheless Lemke knew that this man, in his middle thirties with hair to his shoulders, waved like a woman's, was the man he needed. Franz Halder wrote for *Die Welt* and *Der Spiegel* and was a regular contributor to *The Times* and *Le Figaro.* Although he was not aware of the fact, he had been chosen most carefully for this meeting.

'So, Herr Lemke, your message said you wanted to see me urgently.'

'Another whisky before we start?'

Halder didn't speak, he just pushed forward his glass on the table. As Lemke replaced the whisky bottle he looked intently at the man opposite.

'Can I ask you, Herr Halder, your views on the current NATO situation?'

Halder laughed and raised his eyebrows.

'The Warsaw pact has a three-to-one superiority over NATO in almost every field—arms and men. We Germans and the Americans bear the brunt of the NATO effort.' He shrugged. 'But this is common knowledge.'

'You think the Americans will stay in NATO?'

'God, yes. They moan and groan about the burden, but they go on. They've deserted South-East Asia, they daren't desert Europe. They may not like their commitments, but they'll stick it out.'

'And West Berlin?'

'The Americans would never back down there. The airlift proved that. And the Russians wouldn't try on anything serious. It would mean war.'

'Did you cover the Vienna meeting of Kruschev and Kennedy?'

'1960, no 1961. Yes, I covered it. Kennedy got a mauling from Kruschev but that was to be expected. Kennedy'd only been President for six or seven months. He was the new boy, I expect Kruschev tried him out for size. Made a few threats.'

'Have you any idea what the threats were?'

'No, but I can guess.'

'Tell me.'

'Oh, more trouble in the Middle-East. Arms to Egypt. Trouble in Indonesia. More funds to anti-American governments in South America. That sort of thing. You've got to remember the Russians were riding very high then. Gagarin with the first space flight. The French fighting it out in Algeria. The Russians had never had it so good.'

Lemke put his arm on a thin, brown, leather brief case and patted it with his hand.

'I have the transcript of that meeting here Herr Halder. That's why I wanted to see you.'

Halder stayed relaxed in his chair and his indifference was not disguised.

'The threats went far beyond what you described, Herr Halder.'

Halder shrugged and half-smiled. 'OK, a new blockade of Berlin.'

Lemke looked intently at the younger man and he spoke slowly and clearly.

'The threat was war, Herr Halder, if the Americans didn't give up West Berlin.'

Halder was used to revelations, used to being pumped and manipulated, used to exaggeration.

'A mis-translation maybe or a misunderstanding.'

'Do you speak Russian, Herr Halder?'

'No.'

'What I have here is the original transcript. It's not a copy, a facsimile, or a photostat. It is number nineteen of the transcripts supplied to the members of the Praesidium. I have a notarized translation by Professor Johann Abel. His original signature is on this copy of the translation.'

Halder was very still for a few moments and then he sat up and leaned forward with his hand outstretched. Lemke shook his head.

'I want your word, Herr Halder, that if I show this document you will either publish the information immediately, or forget it. And forget this interview.'

'Herr Lemke, I am told a hundred secrets in a month. If I were not professional and discreet I should be reporting births, deaths and marriages.'

Lemke opened the flap on his brief-case and pulled out two sets of papers. One set was on thick grey paper fastened with a brass split-pin and these Lemke pushed across the table. He seemed to take his hand off them reluctantly.

'This is the actual document. This purple stamp has the date, the Praesidium member's number and the initials of the Praesidium Secretary-General. And here,' he turned over about six pages, 'this is the signature of the member. I emphasize that this is the original document.' Halder followed the explanation and had no doubt that the document was genuine. It even had an odour about it that was Russian. A smell like mothballs. The signature was in brown ink, ornate and artistic. He looked across at Lemke and nodded, as if agreeing the document's authenticity. 'May I see the translation?'

Lemke drew back the original and tucked it carefully into the brief case. He looked briefly at the other papers and passed them across. As Halder took them, Lemke said: 'You'll see that each page is on the printed paper of Professor Abel's Übersetzungsbüro. Each page is signed at the foot by Abel himself, and dated. You will see that there is a photograph stapled to each sheet, of the relevant section of the original document.'

Halder read carefully through the text, sometimes turning back to re-read a line or two. It was nearly fifteen minutes later when he leaned in his chair and stared at Lemke. Lemke sat silent.

'It's incredible.'

Lemke came back quickly.

'What part is incredible?'

'The whole damn thing. I just can't believe it.'

Lemke's face looked sharp with anger.

'You mean you think it is not authentic?'

'Good God, no. I said I *can't* believe, not that I don't believe it.'

'And what are the main points in your view?'

'That Kruschev was mad enough to threaten to go to war with the United States. That it should be about West Berlin. And that Kennedy didn't tell him to go to hell.'

'As you said, Kennedy was the new boy.'

'Oh yes, oh yes, but he was a very experienced politician. And he was the President of the most powerful nation on this planet. To say to Kruschev that he would consider what he had said was pathetic. It showed he was scared.'

'Those are the people we look to for our defence, Herr Halder—the Americans.'

But as Lemke had expected, the philosophizing was over and Halder was the professional journalist again. He pointed to the documents.

'I'll pay whatever you're asking for those.'

Lemke smiled and shook his head.

'There's only one arrangement I will agree to.'

'And what's that?' There was no disguising Halder's eagerness.

'I have in my case the same documents but with the Praesidium member's number and signature omitted. If you give me your word that they will never be mentioned or used and that the information will be published immediately then you have the exclusive rights. I do not want to be quoted as your source.'

'And nobody else has this material?'

'Nobody.'

'The Foreign Ministry?'

'No.'

'The Chancellor?'

'No.'

'The BND?'

'Nobody.'

'There have been rumours about some sort of revelation for a couple of months in Bonn. Is this what they referred to?'

'The Gehlen organization had got wind of an unsatisfactory meeting in Vienna. They tried to pursue it further. They got nothing. There were stories on these lines but they were not only incredible but unsupported.'

Halder stood up. 'I shall be in your debt, Herr Lemke. I agree to the conditions.'

Lemke pulled back the papers. Took out a fresh set in a plastic folder and handed them to the journalist.

'Would you like to check the text with the set you have just read?'

Halder shook his head smiling. 'No, that won't be necessary. And again, my thanks.'

Long after Halder had left, Lemke sat at the table thinking. Passing over the information was the equivalent of pressing a button. It started a machine that would not stop until the operation was ended, be it with success or disaster. Everything would depend on how other people would interpret the clues. The views would range from those of explosive experts, through politicians, to the man in the street.

Chapter 18

By four o'clock that afternoon Lowe was standing in a maze of plastic coils that looked like oversize spaghetti. Each coil was neatly tied and labelled. There were eighteen coils gathered into two separate areas with nine coils apiece. At the end of each white plastic tube was a 90° elbow with a 24-inch tube at the outlet end. At the far end of each tube it snaked into a small plastic cylinder that looked like a motor car distributor. With each cylinder was an old-fashioned stone water bottle.

Mills, passing through, had asked the purpose of the water bottles. Lowe had explained carefully that the phial of liquid gas had to be above 20° centigrade to gasify and that the cylinder would be inserted in the bottle necks and the bottles themselves placed in a plastic bowl with water at the correct temperature. Rochford had come in on the end of the explanation and when Mills walked through to his own small office room Rochford went with him.

'Have you thought what we do afterwards, David?'

'After what?'

'After these guys are dead.'

'When they're dead we go . . . We'll phone their two numbers and if there is no reply we'll assume that the operation's over.'

'Say one survives?'

'So what. He won't carry on on his own.'

'OK. So they're all dead. Who finds them? And how do they avoid being affected by the gas?'

'We'll phone the police and warn them.'

'You phone the police and say there are seventeen dead men on the first floor of the Müller-Haus in Rathausstrasse? Go careful there's a lethal gas in there? It's called Charlie fourteen?'

'Give Lowe a shout.'

Lowe came in and almost stood to attention.

'How long do the effects of this gas hang around? How soon can we go in afterwards?'

'Inside an hour under normal conditions. Even one body in that area would quickly absorb all the gas. We're only putting in minute quantities. If you want to go in quicker I can get access into the air-conditioning circuit and bring down the room temperature very low and we could be in in a matter of minutes.'

Mills looked at Rochford who nodded.

'OK, Mr Lowe. You carry on.'

Rochford exhaled and leaned against the wall.

'What do we do about Tiebert?'

'I want to deal with him, Pierce.'

'You realize he's one of the two exceptions. Neither he nor Lemke will be in the apartment block. What do you think their reactions will be when nothing happens?'

'I'd guess that Tiebert won't give a damn. He's an administrator and paymaster. He's got businesses so life goes on.'

'What about Lemke?'

Mills pursed his lips and shrugged.

'Different sort of man but the same applies. It's not the end of the world. I'd say he'll keep his head down. Maybe we give him a warning not to play games again.'

'I'd recommend we take Munsel's advice on him.'

'Let's find him.'

Munsel was sitting with the girl in Mills' old room. The girl was playing patience at the small table and Munsel was making notes in his diary.

'We'd like a conference, Otto.'

Munsel nodded and stood up. They went into the main

operations room. As they sat down one of the radio operators signalled to Mills to come over. As Mills sat on the chair beside him the operator pointed at the spare headphones. Mills slid the jackplug into the twin fitting and as he put on the headphones there was a blare of Morse. He turned the small control on the right-hand earpiece and the sound came down to normal. It was far too fast to read and Mills saw that the tape recorder was turning and the recording light was on. There were pulses of short bursts and then after a few minutes there was the hiss of the carrier wave and then the silence of empty air. Mills took off the phones and the operator pushed back one ear-piece.

'Did you hear that, sir? There have been bursts on that frequency since mid-afternoon today. The strength's terrific, must be within five to six miles of here and a red-hot transmitter. It's not far from our frequency and there's something queer about it.'

'What way queer?'

'We've been monitoring the BND wavelengths continuously and passing the recordings back to London. They're fast readable Morse and we've taken them down for London to decode. We've monitored all the short-wave transmissions from Nord Deutscher Rundfunk. They're using two unauthorized frequencies but the traffic's in clear on all seven frequencies. That stuff you heard needs high-grade equipment and high-grade operators. It's typical high-grade espionage traffic.'

'Might be our friends in Rathausstrasse.'

'We've done hand-held tests there two days running, and there's nothing going out at all. We had your descriptions of their radio sets, that you got from Fräulein Munsel, but we've identified those. They're just old Wehrmacht armoured vehicle transceivers. They couldn't put out a signal like that. They'd be doing well if you got a low-grade voice signal at three hundred yards.'

'What d'you want to do then?'

'I'd like an RAF jet to take these tapes to London, sir.'

'OK. I'll sign the chit. You know who to contact?'

'Squadron Leader Waring isn't it, sir?'

'That's it.'

As the signals sergeant started to unlace the tape, Mills called from the doorway.

'What do you think it is, Evans?'

The young man turned round slowly, smoothing the yellow tape-lead on to the spool as he looked at Mills.

'Just a guess, sir. It sounds like a Russian transmission to me.'

'You ever monitored them before?'

Evans nodded. 'Yes, sir. We sometimes relieve the unit that monitors their stuff in London. From the Embassy and the Trade Mission place in Highgate.'

Mills opened his mouth to speak, hesitated then closed his mouth, nodded, and walked out of the room.

Munsel and Rochford were in the smaller office talking. Mills gave them the signals memo. Rochford lit a cigarette.

'That could mean two things.'

'Like what?'

'They could have a team here trying to knock off Lemke's boys or they could be acting as unofficial long-stops to make sure we do our stuff. Are your people in London keeping Moscow informed?'

'I don't know. Doesn't seem likely to me.'

'They passed stuff to your people way back to get it started.'

'The BND must be monitoring them too. Same as they'll be monitoring us. They couldn't break our code inside a year. The Russians have almost closed down in West Germany. The Germans were after them tooth and nail. That's why they passed stuff to us because they weren't 'live' themselves. What d'you think, Otto?'

Munsel had got up while they were talking and hands deep in his trouser pockets he was walking slowly around, his head down in thought. He looked up slowly.

'As soon as we get into the ground-floor apartments at

the Müller-Haus I think I'd better have a closer look at Lemke and you'd better do your check on Tiebert's safe. I can probably help the team when we ask the people in the ground floor apartments to move out.' He smiled a little. 'I've still got that German official look.'

Mills walked back to his old room to spend a few moments with the girl. He had only been there a few minutes when there was a knock on the door. It was Munsel and he leaned casually against the door-frame, his hands still in his pockets.

'Tell me, David. They brought you back in specially for this job. SIS I mean?'

'They'd got it lined up already. I don't know that it was specially for this. They hoped that I might influence you to help.'

'And Pierce? He's not full-time CIA, is he?'

'He was, but he hasn't been full-time for some years.'

Munsel looked thoughtful and then smiled at the girl.

'You'll be glad when this is all over my love.'

She nodded and looked fondly at the two men.

'Yes, but it's nice to be with you both.'

And Munsel had left them to themselves.

Mills decided to take the girl for a walk and they left the house at about eight o'clock. They took a taxi at Ost-Weststrasse to Pöseldorf, and ate at one of the small cafés facing the Alster park. A gaggle of sailing dinghies were heading for the moorings by the ferry station, and the gusty evening wind laid them over despite agile young crews stretched out on their trapezes. Motor cruisers were tying up for the night and family dogs lay comfortably on cabin roofs watching their human beings at work. Wealthy businessmen who were waited on hand and foot at home and office, stood bent over mops as they cleaned down teak-laid decks.

They were halfway through their meal when the girl put her hand on his. He looked across at her and smiled. 'You don't have to marry me, David. It's made me feel good that you asked me.'

'You got cold feet?'

She shook her head smiling. 'You know I haven't but I'm afraid of adding to your worries right now.'

He raised his glass of wine to her and she raised hers back, waiting.

'To the day, sweetie.'

'You don't like Germans, do you?'

He put his glass down slowly.

'Whatever made you say that?'

'Something daddy said.'

'Tell me.'

'He said I would have to remember that you'd seen the Germans at their worst. During the war and after the war, and now you were dragged back to deal with the same sort of people again. And once more they're Germans.'

'And Americans too.'

'Daddy said you've got a saying in English. The only good German is a dead German. Is he right?'

Mills frowned and shrugged.

'Yes, it's true, but people say stupid things in the heat of wars.'

'And it won't make any difference to us?'

He laughed and shook his head.

'Of course not. When shall we get married?'

She smiled and put her head on one side to look at him. 'As soon as you want.'

'OK. As soon as this is all over. A few days more.'

'You were there when my father and mother were married, weren't you?'

'Yes. It seems a long, long time ago.'

'Could we get married there?'

'At your grandfather's place?'

'Yes.'

'I had the feeling that things are not too good between them.'

'My grandfather was angry that daddy wouldn't play

politics when he worked for the Government. Said he should be more patriotic. And for my grandfather that means hating the British, the Americans and the Russians.'

'He's hardly likely to welcome me then.'

'Oh yes, he would. You were the only thing they agreed about.' She laughed. 'My grandfather said you should have been a German, you didn't deserve to be English.'

'OK. Well we'll see what your father says. If he says yes then that's what we'll do.'

It was ten-thirty when they got back to the house. For Mills it was like coming back to prison.

There was a sheaf of reports on the trestle table and Mills sat down to read them. The first was a note from Rochford that they planned to attempt the entry to the Müller-Haus at 6 a.m. the following morning. Then there was page after page of details of broadcasts from Paris, London, Hamburg, Bonn, Berlin and Moscow. They all covered reports of the Kruschev-Kennedy meeting and the threats made by the Russian leader. Commentators pointed to the fact that Kennedy had not walked out of the meeting. The Voice of America and the American Forces Network had claimed that the report was spurious, and Washington had made no comment. A NATO spokesman had pointed out that the number of troops in West Berlin was now thirty per cent greater than when the meeting took place. There had not been time for European opinion to express itself except in guarded terms. As Mills sat there reading other signals and reports, further extracts of comments came through. The White House had issued a statement that 'at no time had it ever been considered that troops in Berlin should be withdrawn or substantially reduced'. Moscow made no comment but made the original report its second news item on broadcasts in twenty-seven languages. In the House of Commons the Speaker had refused permission for an immediate debate. The US Ambassador to London was quoted as saying, 'We're still goddam there and there ain't been no goddam war, so who's bluffing who?' The grammar was forgiven because he was a Texan and much loved, and by midnight his quote was the banner headline on the first editions of every British national daily.

Mills settled down on a camp-bed and as he pulled a sleeping bag up to his shoulders he tried to push out of his mind that tomorrow was going to be a terrible day. Whichever way it went there were men right now, spending, or wasting, their last hours alive. His last thought was to wonder why he had not seen Munsel.

They were all awake at 4 a.m. The first pair were already dressed in their uniforms and boiler-suits. Munsel looked tired and pale as he rehearsed the procedures. Lowe and the chemist were making a final check of all the joints in the plastic pipes, and the two gas containers sat ominously in one of the coils. At 5.30 the van picked them up. It was in the official Hamburger Gasworks livery of yellow and black.

At the Müller-Haus the first family were awoken and accepted Munsel's explanations without question. They packed a few things in cases, a taxi was called, and one of the 'company staff' accompanied them to a hotel on Holzdamm. Lowe and his team were assembling the plastic pipe before they left.

The second family were not so easily convinced. They wanted to stay until the repairs were carried out. Munsel played the irate official and quoted an official ordinance granting entry to various services like gas and sewage. At the stage when he took out a note-book to record their refusal they grudgingly submitted. They too were escorted to a hotel. They were given a choice and opted for the Esso Motel.

Mills, Rochford and Munsel sat in one of the bedrooms to finalize the day. The pipes would be assembled in both apartments by mid-morning and it was decided to wait until midday before the drilling was started. It would be done by hand and in short sessions, as Lowe needed to make constant measurements to avoid drilling through too far. The noon traffic and activities would provide cover for any audible sound. For two days there had been no outside movement from Lemke's team apart from the two Americans. Mills' surveillance teams were put on special alert for twenty-four hours, and would stay on, to observe reactions after Mills' team eventually left.

The current reports showed that most of the lights went out on the first floor at eleven each night and they had planned for the gas to be released thirty minutes later.

'The first thing we need to decide,' said Mills, 'is our entry to the apartment. We shall have to accept the chemist's opinion on this. He gives us a minimum of thirty minutes before it is completely safe. I've decided we should make it an hour. And unless you can give any good reasons I intend going in alone. When I've checked, I'll come down for Pierce. I only suggest that so that Pierce can give personal confirmation of what happened to his people in Washington. In that time Lowe and his boys can dismantle their apparatus and plug the holes in the ceiling. I've arranged for Sam Wertheim to contact both families at their hotels and to pay their expenses and bills. He will rendezvous with Lowe and the chemist at Bremen and fly back by RAF jet with all their bits and pieces. Any comments?'

It was Rochford who spoke.

'Is anyone going to notify the police?'

'No. The longer we've got to get away, the better.'

'What about Otto?'

Mills looked at Munsel.

'Otto, I'd like you to stay until about ten this evening. We should be safe here after that. What do you want to do after that?'

'I've arranged for Helga to go to Lisbon. There's a plane I can catch at seven tomorrow morning.'

'Where from?'

'Hamburg.'

'No. That won't do, Otto. It's just possible they may

find them quickly and they'll have checks on ports and airports in fifteen minutes. You've been seen up here and spoken to various people. You'd better come with me.'

'How are you going out?'

'D'you know Heide?'

'The village up the coast road to the frontier?'

'That's it. Well if you turn left there, there's a small road that goes right down to the sea at a village called Büsum. I've arranged for a chopper to pick us up there on the sands.'

'Who's us?'

'Pierce, Jutta, and you, if you agree. You can fly on to Lisbon from London.'

'What about Tiebert and Lemke?'

'I'm going to see to Tiebert this afternoon, after that I'll pick up Jutta, come back here and pick up you two. The rest of the boys are going to one of the Royal Navy boats at Bremerhaven.'

'And that leaves Lemke.'

'OK. Let's leave him.'

Munsel shook his head.

'I think he's the key man. He matters most.'

'He's not going to try this game again after this little trip.'

'I think you're wrong, David. What time is your helicopter?'

'Six tomorrow morning. The pilot will give us thirty minutes overlap for accidents.'

'Can I have a car?'

'Sure. We've got two spare Volkswagens.'

'Let us say I investigate Lemke and I meet you on the sands at Büsum.'

Mills hesitated and looked at Rochford who looked back at him deadpan.

'OK, Otto. I'll give you the map reference. But you can't go wrong: it's on the sands and it's where they have the horse racing. It'll just be light so you can't miss us.'

* * *

At midday Mills took the coast road to Blankenees. It was slower but it was beautiful. A big liner was coming up the Elbe with its paint gleaming in the afternoon sun. Two stubby tugs trapped its massive bulk to hold it steady on the incoming tide. The debris of a working river coated its white Plimsoll line and passengers lined the sides. Away in the background a big sign said 'Deutsche Werft' and the rust-red structures of the repair docks looked like metal sculptures in the golden light.

At Blankenese itself he stopped the car and sat looking at the small fishing boats plunging and swinging to their metal buoys. There were faint shouts from children playing on the narrow strip of sand in front of the breakwater and the sparse bushes bent and sprang back in the wild gusts of wind. The good citizens' houses sprawled along the hills and ended in a foam of white stucco along the sea road. Behind the hills there were the big woolly cumulus clouds of summer, the wind was too low to reach them and they were as still as if they were painted on the deep blue sky. It was a day for girls in bikinis and naked babies making castles in the sand, not for what Mills and the others had to do. For a moment he closed his eyes and touched his face to the cool glass of the car window, then almost automatically he started the engine and let in the clutch. He turned right and went up past the park and into the maze of residential roads.

He stopped the car and switched on the walkie-talkie and called the surveillance team watching Tiebert's house. There had been no callers apart from two tradesmen delivering bread and groceries. The American combination-lock identifying device had worked well but they had ended with two different combinations. It was a differential combination-lock with a double protection of alternating combinations. He noted the two series of numbers and told them he would be along in ten minutes. They should only come to his assistance if he was in the house more than an hour, unless he called them on the walkie-talkie.

He glanced briefly at the two men in the big black

Mercedes as he walked past. They ignored him but he saw the lips moving of the man behind the wheel as he reported Mills' movements back to the control room.

The wide gates of Tiebert's garden were open but he saw the flick of reaction from the electronic sensor as he walked in. He followed the gravel path round the side of the house and turned into the concrete courtyard at the rear. It looked smaller in daylight but he noticed that the glass in the door had been replaced and the wires had been joined and taped. He stood for a moment then pressed the bell-button firmly. He could hear no responding bell inside the house. But a few moments later a speaker grated in the porch above his head.

'Yes. Who is it?'

'A message from Herr Lemke.'

There was a moment's hesitation and then:

'Where are you from?'

'From Rathausstrasse.'

'Wait.'

Mills saw someone approach the door on the other side and then as the white distorted face showed through the small panes of glass he heard bolts drawn and chains released, and an electronic switch was moved. The door opened about a foot and it was Tiebert, wearing an old silk dressing-gown and worn leather slippers. He had a glass in his hand and a newspaper tucked under the same arm. The pale fleshy face was suspicious, and the bulging eyes slowly absorbed his visitor. The loose lips were open and the big belly rose and fell under the dressing gown as he breathed slowly and heavily. He looked a far cry from the youth who had sat at the farmhouse table dressed in a sergeant's uniform, trying to bluff his way out of a tight corner. Mills saw only the vaguest resemblance and he hoped the reverse applied. But there was suspicion in the watery eyes, and as it registered with Mills the door was closing. It still had four inches to go and as his foot went down the door made contact and sprang back, knocking Tiebert's glass from his hand. There was a telephone on a table in the passage and Tiebert reached out for it. His hand had closed round it before he saw the gun in Mills' hand. He lifted his hand from the telephone as if it were hot, and he shuffled backward till his huge bulk was against the wall. His head sent a framed picture rattling, and his arms were half raised defensively.

'Wh' . . . What is it? What do you want?'

Mills gestured with the gun towards the living-room and Tiebert shuffled across the parquet floor and then trod cautiously in the thick pile of the living-room carpet.

'Sit down, Lerner.'

At the sound of that name the protuberant eyes half-closed and he looked up apprehensively at Mills' face as he lowered himself into the fat armchair. Then with his arms on the arms of the chair he leaned forward.

'I don't know you. Why do you call me Lerner?'

'Because you're Max Lerner. Jailed for two years for trying to pass as a British soldier and operating on the black market.'

Tiebert's hand flew to his mouth in surprise and then he pointed.

'You're not a German. You're Mills. You arrested me.' He wiped his wet mouth with the back of his hand. 'That's all over. All done with. You cannot come in my house.' He struggled to stand up and Mills shoved him back.

'Where's the girl?'

'Upstairs. She's asleep.' He looked up quickly at Mills' face. 'Why don't you go up and see her. She'll give you a good time. We've got no quarrel now. The war's over a long time ago.'

'What are the telephone numbers at Rathausstrasse?'

Tiebert's jaw dropped, and he leaned back slowly in his chair. There were beads of sweat on the big smooth forehead. His voice was almost a whisper.

'They said you'd been to see Munsel. I didn't believe them.'

'The telephone numbers, Lerner.'

Tiebert closed his eyes as if to shut out what was happening. His hands were trembling.

'They'll kill me if I tell you.'

Mills brought down the gun butt on Tiebert's knee and he gasped with pain. He cried out pathetically.

'The numbers are in the book—in the telephone directory. Under the old names—Frau Lotte Steiner and Dieter Hoffer—Müller-Haus—Rathausstrasse.'

'OK. Now open the safe.'

'What safe is that?'

The stupid amateurish attempt only annoyed Mills.

'Open the safe, Lerner—and quick.'

Tiebert struggled to his feet and went to the office door. He leaned against the door frame for a moment, his head bowed, and then he walked slowly to the desk. He leaned over and swung back the painting. He put his hand to his head as he tried to work it out. He didn't turn when Mills spoke.

'It's the one that starts zero nine four anti-clockwise.'

The fat hand closed over the brass knob and turned and counter-turned. Then he hesitated for a moment and swung open the door. Mills waved him to the swivel-chair and it creaked as he let himself down.

Mills cleared the safe of its contents and laid them on the desk. There were about two hundred thousand Deutschmarks in high denominations. A thick wad of hundred dollar notes, and a small chamois leather bag heavy with British sovereigns. There were several passports with Tiebert's photograph and different identities. Two were German and the others Argentine, British and Irish. There were deeds to various properties, including the Hotel Helga. And nothing more.

'Where are the photographs, Lerner?'

And Mills had turned towards Tiebert as he spoke. He saw the quick glance and the look of sudden hope. As he swung he saw the girl standing at the door. She was naked and she had a gun in her hand.

'I don't know your name, little girl, but a trained marksman couldn't hit me with that thing. So put it down on the floor very carefully and stand quite still.'

The girl looked across at Tiebert.

'Shall I shoot him, Herr Tiebert?'

There was a noise like a hose coming off a tap from the silencer on Mills' gun and the door frame near the girl splintered so that chips of painted wood flew in the air. The girl lowered the gun, then stooped gracefully and laid it on the floor. She stood up slowly and looked at Mills. She was very young, with the golden skin that some Eurasians are lucky enough to be born with. The long black hair coiled on her shoulders and her eyes were a deep velvety brown. She stood, aware of Mills' eyes on her, but seemingly unembarrassed. Her neat breasts were no bigger than apples but her hips flowed softy into the long shapely legs. When his eyes went down to the firm flat oval of her belly she smiled and thrust out her hips in obvious invitation.

Mills had made Tiebert go up to the girl's room with him and he'd told her to dress. He had picked up the pearl-handled gun. It was a .22 and the safety catch was rusted into the 'on' position. He slid out the feed chamber and tucked it into his pocket. When the girl was dressed he'd walked them both to the end of the corridor and checked the toilet. There was a small window at the top of the wall and a low flushing suite. He stood aside and motioned the girl inside.

'Just sit quiet. They'll let you out in an hour. If you make any noise there'll be trouble for you, and for him.' He pointed the gun at Tiebert. He locked the door on her and put the key in his pocket.

'Now Tiebert. The photographs.'

'I don't understand. What photographs?'

Mills' open hand crashed against Tiebert's face, he staggered and put out his arm to support himself against the wall. The dressing-gown had fallen open and his hand clasped his gross belly as he fought for his breath. Mills stood silent. He looked at his watch. There were still thirty minutes to go. Tiebert was trembling violently and as Mills looked at him he gasped: 'Please, please, take the money. Take it and go. Just leave me.'

Mills' left hand went to Tiebert's throat and his head crashed against the wall. His body seemed to deflate and he slumped to his knees and fell forward. All Mills' pent-up anger swept over him. He dropped the gun and straddling Tiebert he clutched both his shoulders and pounded his head again and again on the parquet floor. Tiebert screamed and Mills' hand clamped over his mouth pulling his jaws apart. 'Are you going to show me where they are?' he gasped. Tiebert nodded his head as best he could and Mills sat back on the flabby belly and slowly got to his feet. He stood over Tiebert and looked down at him. 'Where are they?' Tiebert feebly waved an arm. 'Outside . . . outside.' 'In the laundry building or the garages?' Tiebert nodded but his eyes were closed and he couldn't speak. 'Which one? The garages?' Tiebert shook his head and there was blood coming from his mouth.

Chapter 19

Mills picked up the gun and ran down the stairs. The rear door was still open and he crossed the concrete square to the long narrow block that housed the laundry. The door was unlocked and as he went in he guessed he wanted the room he'd seen at the end. The room without windows. It was probably a darkroom. The door was solid, painted a dark green. He tried the brass knob but it didn't give. He put his shoulder to the door but it didn't shift. He stepped back and levelled his gun at the lock area, as he fired there was the crashing impact of the slug, the whine of a ricochet and the whir of flattened lead as it flew past his head. The door was metal and the slug had barely chipped the paint.

Mills went back upstairs in the house to where he had left Tiebert. The man was on his knees, his hands clasping the banisters in an attempt to stand up. Mills snatched his head back by the sparse grey hair.

'Where are the keys?'

Tiebert's eyes were glazed and there was dark dried blood covering his chest to his belly. He shuddered as he tried to speak.

'Clothes . . . bedroom . . . pocket.'

In the main bedroom there was a blue suit laid out on the bed and on a side table was a wallet, coins and a bunch of keys.

The key seemed to wind round loosely in the brass knob, but on the third complete turn Mills felt it engage the tumblers. His hand felt for the light switch in the darkness of the room. As he pressed it down the lights came on and there was the rush of an air-conditioner starting up.

It was a small room about three metres by two and along one wall was all the paraphernalia of a darkroom. Trays, dishes and beakers. Shelves of chemicals. A second timer and a beautiful red and grey Durst 601 enlarger. A tap dripped in the double sink. But it was the small device that sat in solitary splendour on the enlarger's white baseboard that caught his eye. It looked like a small primitive microscope in grey plastic. Half covering the main tube was a slide that had been pushed back up the tube to accommodate the light from the enlarger lens. It was light, cheap to produce and could be disassembled to fit inside a small tin of talcum powder. And they were standard issue as micro-dot readers. Standard issue for the KGB.

On the wall behind him was a grey, metal-clad radio with 4-inch diameter tuning dials. As his hand turned one, the gearing moved the other dials and they were so geared that a one degree movement on the first dial moved the last dial through 90 degrees. The other controls had paper labels. He put his hand over the ventilating panel but the set was cold. There were special-frequency crystals in their small ovens in plastic boxes, ranged along a wooden shelf. A large Tandberg reel-to-reel tape-recorder stood in a vertical position alongside the transceiver and there was a pair of wires linked to the radio facia. There was tape on the recorder. On the pine desk were three one-time code pads. One was missing half its leaves. A digital clock and calendar hummed quietly as the green display figures changed every tenth of a second.

He found the photographs carelessly thrown in one of the drawers beside the sink. He counted carefully, 8 strips of three negatives each. The Rolleiflex was in the drawer and he undid the back but it was empty. He pulled over one of the smaller developing trays and touched each strip to the pilot light of the sink-heater. The film burned slowly and when it was too hot to hold he let it burn itself out in the dish. The polythene scorched and gave off an acrid bitter-smelling smoke. When all the film was destroyed he burnt all the prints. They were ten by eights, and as they smouldered he tried not to look. It wasn't within his power, and the scenes etched themselves irrevocably on his mind's eye. The excitement on the girl's face was undeniable and in some shots she was smiling into the camera ignoring the men enjoying her body, in an obvious attempt to excite the photographer. Why any pretty girl should want to attract Tiebert, except for money, was beyond Mills' comprehension. Slowly the pile of charred paper increased. When the last corner of the last print curled as the small flame ate it away he turned on the tap. He broke it all up to a grey solution and flushed it down the sink. Then he lifted the walkie-talkie from his top pocket and called the surveillance team. One of them joined him a few minutes later.

'Can you use this thing inside the house here and still get central control?' He was pointing at the man's walkie-talkie.

'Yes, but I'll have to use yours, our power's getting very low.'

'Is Taffy on the other end?'

'Was a few minutes ago. They can put him on even if he's been relieved.'

'Before you do that have a look at this radio equipment. When you go on next, describe it very briefly to Taffy and tell him I want him out here with one of the small vans. I want it taken back to control. All of it. Code pads, crystals, the lot. And this as well.' And he turned and pointed at the micro-dot reader.

The signals sergeant reached for Mills' walkie-talkie, pressed the button and held it to his mouth.

'Ar hyd y nos . . . Ar hyd y nos . . .'

As on many walkie-talkie teams used for overseas surveillance, the operators were Welsh speaking, the line from the old Welsh hymn was much used as a call sign.

When he had finished he handed Mills the walkie-talkie.

'Thanks. There's a girl upstairs, locked in the loo. I was going to loose her out but we'd better keep her tucked away until it's all over. Here's the key. Give her food and keep her out of mischief. Tiebert's upstairs too. He's not very well. Won't cause any trouble but keep him away from the phones. We'll have to . . .' He broke off, his hand in mid-gesture. 'My God, my God, what a fool, it's not just the radio.' He ran from the room with the sergeant following. He found Tiebert in the bathroom sitting on the toilet seat—his head and shoulders bent forward. As he grasped Tiebert's shoulders the huge bulk of the man slowly leaned over and fell with a sickening thud that rat- ted the glasses on a shelf. Tiebert had fallen on his side, and Mills struggled in the narrow space alongside the bath to turn him face upwards. As the heavy body came round he knew from the cold clammy flesh that Tiebert was dead. His face was contorted in pain and his stiff arm showed how he had died. His hand was clutching his heart. The sergeant noticed the swollen face, the purple swellings each side of Tiebert's throat and the puffy mass of Tiebert's right eye. He reckoned that Mills probably didn't realize his own strength.

Mills looked up from where he crouched over Tiebert's body. 'Can you contact the team at the Müller-Haus?'

'Not direct sir. But control could give me a link.'

'Get 'em then.'

Rochford was on net about five minutes later.

'You want me, David?'

'Both of you. You and Otto. There's something funny going on, Pierce. This operation may not be what we think it is. Tell Otto I want him to get his stuff on Lemke from control and I'll meet you both, where you are now, in half an hour.'

Mills could hear the girl laughing with the signals ser- geant upstairs, and he called up that he was leaving.

Rochford and Munsel were waiting for him at the Müller-Haus apartment. The long plastic tubes were snaking from every room to the emission point in the kitchen. The same network had been fixed in both of the two ground floor apartments. As he walked through to the living-room Lowe asked to speak to him.

'I've drilled through all the ceilings now sir. The holes are small diameter, only about half an inch. I've left the last eighth of an inch until you give the word. I've improved the plan. We're putting through a thin metal tube so it will be virtually impossible for any of the people upstairs to notice what we've done. They might just have twigged a half inch hole before we got the tube lined up.'

'How long will you need to go ahead?'

'We've tried it on dry runs and it averages out at seventeen minutes for each apartment.'

'And from that point on how long from when we press the button till it works.'

'When you give us the word for the final drilling I'm going to turn up the wick on the central-heating. When you tell us to discharge the gas it will take two minutes to fill the pipes and about two minutes more to build up enough pressure to go through the needle tubes.'

'And after that?'

Lowe shook his head.

'It's virtually instantaneous. It'll be over in seconds whatever they do.'

'And to take down all the pipes and stuff?'

'It isn't that that'll take the time, sir. I've got to get our room temperatures right down. Windows and doors open, and heating off, it'll take the best part of twenty minutes. I'll plug the holes in about thirty minutes and have the pipe cut up into short lengths in about an hour. There's a massive boiler in the basement and I can get it all on there in four loads. Say another twenty minutes.'

'And no residual dangers?'

'Absolutely none, sir. We've checked that very carefully.'

'OK. I'll let you know when I want them knocked out

and you can work your timing back from that. See me in an hour.'

He waved Rochford and Munsel into the bedroom they were using as a planning centre.

'Otto, you showed me a summary of a report you'd done on Lemke. You got it here?'

Munself reached across the bed for his brief case and took out a manilla file cover. He leafed through the pages and brought out a couple which were stapled together. He glanced at it briefly and handed it to Mills.

Mills fished for a pencil in his jacket and then laid the papers on the dressing table as he read through them carefully. He marked certain items as he went.

His face was grim as he walked back to sit in one of the cane bedroom chairs. He looked from Rochford to Munsel.

'We've got our sums all wrong. Everything we've done was correct but none of it's what we think it is. Back at Tiebert's place he'd got a room in one of the out-buildings. No windows, heavy metal door, fancy lock and so on. When I got in there it was all rigged up as a darkroom. So OK. Except for a couple of things. There was a KGB standard micro-dot reader. Been used recently, using the light from the enlarger. The second thing was a radio rig. High-powered, very latest and complete with tape-recorder. Remember that report of high-speed burst transmissions in the Hamburg area? That was friend Tiebert. It didn't click with me at first but then I remembered. When he was with Fremde Heere Ost he was a radio operator.

'Then look at this stuff on Lemke. Speaks fluent Russian. It says "joined clandestine training school for officers in 1934". All those schools were in Russia. Next item. He was arrested in 1945 after the capitulation—in Berlin. I'd bet everything I have that he was arrested by the Russians. And lastly. His family estates and business were around Magdeburg, and that's in the Russian Zone. So where did he get the dough for his investments?'

He stopped to let it sink in. It was Rochford who spoke first.

'You saying this is a KGB mob?'

Mills shook his head and shrugged. 'I don't think so. I think these people have been put together by Lemke and Tiebert. Those two are KGB I'm sure of that now. The Germans and Americans in their team all think it's for real.'

'So what's the object? What's the pay-off for the KGB? These people blow up the City Hall. Kill a lot of people. Everybody yells like mad. They find links in the debris to Moscow. So every western politician says look what those bastards have done. So where are the medals for the KGB. Moscow gets exposed and they can forget détente, trade deals and arms limitations as of now. It doesn't hang together, David.'

Munsel leaned back against the pillows on the other bed.

'David's right, Pierce. There are some things that confirm it in my mind. The basic, initial information came from the KGB. Complaints from Moscow to the West German government about ex-Gehlen people operating independently against Warsaw pact countries. Information passed at diplomatic level to the British and the Americans. It stinks of one of those games the KGB loves.'

Rochford stubbed out his cigarette.

'So what do they get?'

'Your analysis was correct except it went too far. Lemke and Tiebert are on the outside of all this. They won't be identified as part of the team. They can provide all the documentation that's needed to show that this was a CIA and Gehlen exercise. They don't have to be named or identified. Some KGB stooge in Washington or Bonn hands over a dossier to his favourite newsman and the balloon goes up. The CIA is discredited along with the United States government. If people think they organized it they'll be rated as thugs, if they think the Americans didn't know they'll say the CIA is uncontrollable. And as for the Germans, all Europe will be glad to believe we've been up to our old tricks again.'

Rochford stood up and walked over to the window. He stood with his hands in his pockets looking out at the busy street. After a long silence he turned and looked at Mills.

'You realize something else, David. My people could have picked some regular CIA man for this, but they didn't. They chose me. An individual they can throw to the wolves if it's all snarled up. And your people didn't pick a regular SIS man, they recruited you. The more I think about it the more I think it's one of the specials from the 'dirty tricks' boys. I think maybe the bastards know it's a KGB frame-up.'

'So what's in it for them, Pierce?'

'Let's work it out, fella. There are CIA people who *would* support an ex-Gehlen mob. There are ex-Gehlen people who'd love another go at the Russians. Both groups would be rocking the boat if we really want détente with the Soviets. So your boys in SIS, and mine in CIA, put on a show of co-operation with the KGB. You and I are shoved in like ferrets down a rabbit hole. There's no big bang. No dead senators in Hamburg City Hall. Just nothing. But there's a few corpses, quietly hushed up with the German authorities. Three or four Yanks, and a dozen or so Germans. But the word gets around in the business. So if you're CIA, and you were playing footsie with any idea of using ex-Gehlen people—well you've had fair warning. And if you're ex-Gehlen fancying a return match with the Russians you've had fair warning too. And then you've got the real nice bit. The KGB are left with egg on their faces. But CIA and SIS have done their good deed. They stopped the action that would get linked with the KGB. They've done what the KGB asked them to do. We go home and collect our pay and a pat on the back, and we're told we've helped keep the peace between the two big boys. The KGB have no revelation to make because there's been no big bang. Lemke can't expose something that's never happened. The KGB will down-grade him fast as a bungler and that's that. Everybody lives happy ever after except the boys upstairs.'

Munsel looked at Mills and waited for him to speak.

'We'll have to deal with Lemke, David, and we'll have to do it quickly. If he finds that Tiebert is dead and that someone's been in there, he'll be gone.'

'What if he goes?'

Rochford chipped in quickly.

'He's the start of the next ball-game in Germany if we leave him. Otto's right: we've got to fix that bastard too. The Moscow Centre might just do their sums right with his detailed information. And our people wouldn't like that.'

Munsel patted one of the pillows to fit his head.

'There's one other indication that your people expected Lemke to be eliminated.'

'What's that?'

'When you signalled London for paratroopers. With those on hand you could have left the people upstairs alive, and sorted it out with the various governments. They wouldn't send them because they want everybody concerned with this eliminated.'

'Us too you mean?'

'No. You two will go back, and they'll shut you up or disown you if you start talking about the KGB playing games. They'll prove it was impossible. But they need you two around as part of the record.'

Mills stood up and looked at his watch.

'Three hours to go, it's eight o'clock. I'll speak to young Lowe and then I'm going back to control. I'll clear up all the stuff there. Give them new orders, pick up Jutta and come back here and we'll talk about Lemke when I get back. I agree. We'll have to finish him.'

He was at the door when he stopped. 'Pierce, there was a girl at Tiebert's place. I thought we could let her go, she's only a kid. The surveillance team are taking her back with the equipment to control. I hadn't found the radio gear when I'd planned to release her.' He looked tired and depressed as he looked across at Rochford. 'Detail one of the team here to dump her. I'd suggest Sammy but I leave it to you. She's only a kid. One of the tarts from Tiebert's hotel. He'll have to take her right out of town. Maybe up to the Danish border.'

Rochford nodded.

'OK. See you.'

Mills stood alone with the girl in the empty house in St Pauli. All traces of its recent occupants had been removed, the furniture was back in place, the festoons of wires and aerials had gone, and the only sounds were from the fishing boats tied up alongside the quay. Very faintly the thin strains of an accordion seeped into the room. The girl put her head on one side and listened intently. After a few moments she smiled up at him.

'Can you hear what they're playing, David?'

He listened, then shook his head.

'It's an old, old song. I've heard mamma sing it when they used to have musical evenings. Sometimes I crept downstairs and sat in the hall and listened. It's really a song for a man to sing. It's called "Dein ist mein ganzes Herz". Richard Tauber used to sing it in English, "You are my heart's delight". Can that be our song, David?'

He smiled and squeezed her hand and tried not to think of the photographs.

'Of course it can. You can sing it to me while *our* children sit on the stairs.'

'Why David, what's the matter?'

And suddenly all his strength had gone. He closed his eyes as the blood drained from his face and the room lurched downwards and round.

'I'll have to lie down Jutta. I'll have to lie down.'

And she had led him to the small bedroom and pulled back the cover from the bed. He lay there with his eyes shut, and she held his hand as he breathed shallowly. There was a mad film in his mind that wouldn't stop. Munsel walking up a ploughed field, his hair waving in the wind.

The young Max Lerner in the farmhouse at Glücksburg, cocky and self-assured. Dead fish lying on a wet green carpet. Whisky pouring into a sink from a plastic bottle. The bright sun and black shadows on the villas in Amalfi. The glare of the neon lights on the Reeperbahn. Three men pushing Lacy in to a car. A fat man lying on a bathroom floor, his chest matted with dried blood and the teeth bared in pain in the swollen battered face. Jutta in the summerhouse smiling at an old man as he handled her big white breasts. A pair of gold cuff-links long since mislaid and an organ playing Elgar. It was like a play that had gone on too long. A saga that showed the players dying, till none were left. He opened his eyes and looked at the girl. The street light from the window set a halo round the blonde head and as he looked at the lovely face he wondered what the end of her story would be. She'd go on after he had gone, but where and how. And he thought of the men in the first floor apartment, and he didn't care about them. He hadn't known them when they were young and at the beginning. They weren't the class of '45.

'What time is it, Jutta?'

'Almost ten. Five before ten.'

'We must go, love. They'll need me there.'

Downstairs as he locked the front door the strength came back, suddenly and for no reason. There were taxis at the Baumwall station. They got out at the end of Rathausstrasse and walked slowly down to the Müller-Haus. There was only an hour to go.

Lieutenant Lowe, Royal Engineers, was standing hands on hips looking up at the ceiling, a stethoscope hung round his neck. When Mills walked in, the young man looked at his watch.

'Sorry about the delay, sir. We're target time plus five minutes. One of my holes came up into metal. A filing cabinet or something like that. All the rest're OK.'

Rochford touched his arm, and when he turned, nodded briefly towards the next room. Mills walked through and Rochford followed.

'How'd you feel about letting Munsel deal with Lemke?'

'On his own, you mean?'

'Yep.'

'No. I'll go with him if he goes at all.'

'He's done some checking. Lemke *was* picked up by the Russians in 1945. The family business *was* taken over by the Russians and is still doing well. They probably paid him well as part of the deal when he was recruited. Apart from that, there are five or six relations of his, still in the Magdeburg area. They're all doing well too. Looks like he's their insurance as well. Sammy's dealt with Tiebert's girl friend. He buried her in a pine-wood just outside a dump called Bad Schwartau, just north of Lübeck.'

'Anybody check her identity?'

' 'Fraid not. No time.'

'Do we know where Lemke is tonight?'

'We sure do. He went to a diplomatic reception for the Jugoslav ambassador at City Hall, and then he drove to a place he owns right outside the city. Seems he's got a country place there in the woods. A town called Friedrichsruh. Big scene for Bismarck I gather. He's buried some place out there.'

'That means we've got to go out there and then come back through the city again.'

'Won't be bad at that time in the morning.'

'Means I've got to leave here with Otto before eleven though.' He paused for a moment. 'Will you look after Jutta for me?'

'You betcha. Any time.'

Chapter 20

Lowe and the chemist were dipping thermometers into the stone water bottles and finally they were satisfied. They synchronized watches and the chemist went off with one bottle for the other apartment. There were eight minutes to go and the temperature in the rooms was almost unbearable. An extension cable had been fitted to the telephone and Lowe sat holding the receiver. He was linked to the other apartment and keeping up a flow of comments and instructions. Rochford, Munsel and Mills had come into the room to watch. At 22.50 Lowe bent forward and lifted the small metal cylinder with its array of connections. He unscrewed the bottle top and still holding the telephone he quietly said, 'Now', and the cylinder slid into the warm water. A silvery film of condensation formed on the top of the cylinder and, as they watched, Lowe started the count-down from thirty seconds. 'Eight—seven—six—five—four—three—two—one—turn,' and he turned the knurled top a whole turn. 'OK Ginger, that's it.' He put down the phone and kept his eyes on his watch. They saw his lips moving as he silently counted. It seemed a long wait but it was only two minutes later when he turned back the top to the closed position. Mills could hear windows being opened and the autumn chill began to take over. When Lowe came back he looked at Mills.

'Technically we could go in now, sir. But I'd prefer another ten minutes.'

Rochford lit a cigarette and whistled softly through his teeth. Munsel had looked up at the ceiling as if aware of what was happening a few feet above their heads. Mills called to Lowe in the next room.

'Mr Lowe, I want you.'

'Sir.'

'Mr Rochford, you and the chemist fellow, will accompany me upstairs. I want photographs of every room and the bodies. I want all four of us to confirm that death has taken place for everyone there. Now send Crowther to see me.'

Crowther looked the soldier he had been.

'Captain Crowther, I want all the radios, apparatus and paraphernalia removed from upstairs. Your men can have fifteen minutes. All documents removed. Anything that could indicate what these people were up to has to be removed. There are crates in bedroom four in this apartment. Everything goes in there and you take it with you to Bremerhaven. You report there to the Senior Royal Navy Officer and he'll tell you what to do. I want two of your men to stay behind with walkie-talkies and the small transceiver. When Mr Rochford and his party leave, the two men will leave the building and continue surveillance of this place until o-seven hundred hours tomorrow morning. They can contact me on our standard frequency but not unless they really need to. Understood?'

'Yes, sir.'

'Has Sammy got back?'

'Yes, sir.'

'Right. Tell Sammy to check into a hotel now. Tomorrow morning he pays the bills for the two families from this place, plus a hundred marks apiece. He leaves them a message with reception that they can go back at four in the afternoon. He goes to the airport and books on a flight to Düsseldorf. At o-eight thirty hours he calls the police. Very short—something like "check the first floor at the Müller-Haus in Rathausstrasse". Then he hangs up. There'll be a message for him at Düsseldorf. OK?'

'OK, sir. The police went to Tiebert's place in Blankenese at eight this evening. Far as we can check it was in response to a call from his wife. She'd tried to phone him and couldn't get an answer. The police doctor came and about ten minutes later an ambulance. No crime squad as far as we could see but our chap had gone by eight-thirty'.

'Where's Colonel Munsel?'

'Talking to his daughter, sir.'

Munsel was cleaning a gun in the small bedroom. He was on his own. He looked up from the gun to Mills' face.

'Jutta tells me you're not feeling too well, David.'

'I'm all right now. A bit over-tired.'

'I gather she wants the wedding to be in her grandfather's chapel.'

'Depends on what you feel, Otto.'

Munsel pushed down the toggle joint and closed the breach of the Luger and laid it on its side on the bed.

'David, there's nothing would make me happier than that Jutta should be married to you. But part of that happiness would be because it would lessen my responsibilities. Are you sure you want to take them over?'

Mills sat down, facing him across the bed.

'We talked about this on the phone, Otto. I hope that being married to me will help her. There'll be problems for both of us. Your support would help a lot. Your approval would help even more—not of me, not of the marriage, but of her.'

Munsel sighed deeply. 'David, she was always beautiful, always lazy. It's easy to get by if you're beautiful, even for a child. I tried to make her compete with her brother. It was stupid, like trying to turn a pear into an apple. It turned out to be disastrous. Anything I can do I will do, but I don't want merely to transfer my unhappiness to you.'

'So you'll speak to the Count?'

'Oh, he'll welcome it. The whole village will be on parade. He has a genuine liking for you.'

'You could have fooled me.'

'That was long ago, David. A time when dignity was bought very dearly.' He smiled. 'Even *he* is older now.'

'Do you know how to get to Lemke's place at Friedrichsruh?'

'Yes, it will take us maybe forty minutes.'

'You'd better get ready, Otto.'

The key to the upstairs flat was a poor fit and it took five minutes to adjust it. As the group stood waiting, the complete silence in the building was oppressive. The lights on the landing seemed dim and naked, the carpets threadbare and the walls unkempt.

Mills turned the key and pushed the door. A body lay across the entrance and it took all Mills' strength to shove its bulk sufficiently aside to squeeze through the opening. He switched on the light. The body was Polanski's and his face was suffused with a reddish-blue fiush, the lips were very bright pink. Mills bent down and pulled the body clear of the door. There were eighteen bodies and it looked as if death had been instantaneous in most cases. Many were in their beds and three were at a table, one of them still had a fork in his hand.

Rochford phoned to the downstairs apartment for the full team to come up, and half an hour later most of the arms and apparatus had been cleared. The detonators and the gelignite had been prepared and labelled with reference numbers for placement. It was Lowe's opinion that there was enough explosive material to have taken out half the City Hall. As the room became innocent of the apparatus and paraphernalia of destruction the whole scene was more and more incongruous. It was strangely Germanic, a story from Grimm of sleeping courtiers without their fairy princess. The unreality was undramatic and it seemed possible that the sleepers would awake or the actors get to their feet when the curtain rose for a round of applause.

Rochford, Lowe, and the biochemist, had made copious notes but Mills looked, and left it at that. Not out of humanity or compunction but from an instinct that the data would never concern him.

Munsel drove the Mercedes with Mills beside him and the big signpost indicated European Highway number 15 and the smaller gave 15 kilometres to Bergedorf. The traffic in Hamburg had been almost as heavy as in the day-time but as they swept over the fly-way across route E4 it thinned out to giant articulateds heading for the East German border and a few long-distance commuters.

Mills closed his eyes and thought of the girl. In maybe four hours they would meet at Büsum and sit in the sand dunes waiting for the helicopter. She'd gone off like a lamb, what he said was always enough. She asked for no reasons, no explanations, that it was what he wanted was enough justification for her.

They were making good time on the big straight road and the villages that flashed past were dark and unlit. The world was asleep. At Bergedorf they took Route 207, the Schwarzenbeker Landstrasse, and the pine woods came down to the edge of the road. The big headlights made the giant trees look like a stage set and Mills saw a badger at the side of the road, turning its striped head from the light. They swung left at Friedrichsruherstrasse, and soon the woods stretched far back on each side of the road. At the first lay-by they pulled in and doused the lights. Mills called up his surveillance team who were still watching Lemke. The little red diodes flickered, then shone. He pressed the button and spoke.

'Hengist calling Horsa, what's the position?'

'Horsa responding. Subject still in house. Was visited by four men, unidentified, at twenty hundred hours. Party stayed thirty-five minutes. One of them patrolled area of house while others inside. Vehicle was black Mercedes 600 limousine version. Registration number unobtainable. Appeared intentionally obliterated. Unable check destination only two on this team. Appeared to be heading Hamburg. Unusual aerial rig. Lights still on in house.'

'Can you give directions from map reference 647 349 Sheet two?'

There was a long silence and some static.

'Carry on due north one kilometre. At wooden bus shelter on right turn first right. Continue point six kilometres and stop, we will contact there.'

Apart from a courting couple in the bus shelter the road was deserted, and when they turned right Mills saw a car headlights flick and die ahead of them. They pulled up facing the Volkswagen and one of the team came over and got in the back seat.

'Evening, sir, or morning I suppose it is. We had a message from control for you about ten minutes ago. Said they were all wrapped up and on their way to Bremerhaven. What d'ye want to know about our bird?'

'Who's in the house apart from Lemke?'

'An old boy, looks about ninety. He'll be no trouble. That's the lot.'

'You see any of the visitors?'

'Not really. I got the impression they didn't want to be seen.'

'You hear them talk.'

'No, we were never that near.'

'How were they dressed?'

'Oh God, let's see now, sort of old-fashioned. Dark coats, dark hats. That's about it. Like old-fashioned gangsters in a 1930 film.'

Mills took a quick glance at Munsel but Munsel didn't respond.

'What's the house like?'

'The locals call it a hunting-lodge but it's a fair-sized place. All on the ground floor. As far as we can see there's a dining-room, a sitting-room and four bedrooms, couple of bathrooms, a kitchen, and that's about it. A double garage.'

'Any protection?'

'No dogs, no electronics, as far as we can see. I don't think he uses it a lot. We checked at a couple of the shops.

About once a month he comes here. Always on his own. Seldom stays more than one night.'

'What car's he got here?'

'None. Came by S-bahn to Aumühle and took a taxi.'

'We'll be going in to see Lemke. One of you'd better patrol the garden for us.'

'It's the next house up on the right. It's the only house on either side till you get to the row of shops. One of us will cover you till you're in and then patrol the garden. How long will you be?'

'Not long. Maybe half an hour.'

There was the scent of lavender as they walked up the path and as they neared the door there was the sound of music. It was one of the Brandenburg Concertos, and the cheerful, lively music seemed ill-fitted to their purpose.

A bell chimed inside as Mills released the button, and almost at once the door was opened. An old man stood there, the light from the hall on his face. It was Munsel who spoke.

'I should like to see Herr Lemke.'

The old man stood hesitating.

'Tell him it's Colonel Munsel.'

A shadow fell across the old man's face and the door opened wide. And there was Lemke himself.

'Come in, Munsel. I've been expecting a visit for some days.'

Lemke stood aside and politely waved them inside.

'And this must be the English gentleman I've heard about.'

The alert eyes looked carefully over Mills' face for a moment, and then led them both through a heavy door to the kind of living-room that was common in expensive Austrian chalets. There was a redwood floor and pine walls. A big log fire blazed in the wide fireplace and its flames reflected and flickered on a display of Dresden figures in a cabinet. There was a comfortable chair drawn up beside the fire and Lemke busied himself arranging two others.

Lemke was wearing a light-weight suit in grey, and a white crew-necked sweater. He looked the unostentatious wealthy man that he was. He needed no paraphernalia to support his obvious authority. He had the natural confidence of a man who was used to giving orders in a quiet voice—just once. He walked over to a plain oak cupboard and brought out glasses and a bottle.

'A brandy while we talk perhaps?'

When they both declined he poured himself a generous helping, waved them to the chairs and sat down.

'So. Let us talk.'

Mills responded quickly. And his face looked grim.

'Just you talk, Herr Lemke.'

Lemke put down his glass, folded his arms defensively but leaned back comfortably in his chair. The pale blue eyes looked at Mills without fear or concern. He looked at the gold watch on his wrist and smiled icily.

'When I have callers at three-thirty in the morning I tend to be a poor conversationalist.'

'Who is controlling this operation at Moscow Centre, Herr Lemke.'

Mills saw the shrewd eyes narrow before Lemke reached for the silver cigarette case. He opened the lid, took out a pale blue cigarette, and carefully lit it. As he put down the onyx lighter he turned to Munsel.

'What's this all about, Otto?'

Munsel spoke slowly and his mouth showed his anger and disgust.

'It's too late to bluff, Lemke. It's all finished now.'

Lemke smiled icily as he looked at the tip of his cigarette.

'Let's establish what we're talking about, Otto, then maybe we *can* talk.'

'Have they told you that Tiebert's dead?'

The eagle's head came round slowly, the eyes like a

vulture's eyes, alert and awaiting a chance to strike. He nodded.

'I had heard that Herr Tiebert had died and that his house in Blankenese had been ransacked. I gather the police are already making inquiries into the possibility of murder.'

'The transmitter has been removed, and the rest of the stuff.'

'Why are you telling me this? What possible interest can it be to me? I hardly knew the man.'

Mills leaned forward and jabbed his hand as he spoke.

'You've met him five times in the last three days. Twice at his brothel in St Pauli. And in the company of two Americans, CIA men named Polanski and Fellows. We have photographs from surveillance teams. Your connection is established. Including your connection with the Müller-Haus apartments in Rathausstrasse.'

Lemke stubbed out his cigarette and reached for another. He ignored Mills and looked at Munsel.

'I am sure you understand that the photographs of your daughter were not taken with my knowledge, nor sent with my approval.'

Mills sensed that even this minor disassociation from Tiebert was the first sign of Lemke's retreat. Munsel didn't reply and after a moment's silence Lemke continued.

'There are things that have to be done, Otto. Things to keep the peace. If a group of men decide that our government's policy towards Moscow is wrong they have the right to protest. We all . . .'

'. . . and the right to kill innocent people, Lemke?'

'Some would say that that is better than making peace with the Bolsheviks.'

Mills put up his hand.

'You're wasting our time, Lemke. You were just using this group. You and Tiebert were exploiting them for the KGB. And it's finished. It hasn't worked.'

Lemke blew out a cloud of blue smoke with his eyes half closed. But Mills didn't wait for him to speak again.

'The team are finished, Lemke. They're all dead. The lot of them.'

Lemke sat up in his chair smiling.

'There was a local news bulletin just finished before you arrived my friend. There was no mention of a mass killing. Sixteen, seventeen men killed? In the heart of Hamburg? Even that lively city would not take that in it's stride.'

'They're dead, Lemke. It's not a bluff.' Munsel's voice was flat and depressed.

Lemke's face was white and drawn, and his voice was harsh.

'So, gentlemen, why are you here?'

'We want to know who's directing it in Moscow.'

Lemke sat still and quiet in his chair as he looked vacantly at the fire. Without turning his head he said, 'You're treading on very dangerous ground, Munsel. Very dangerous indeed.' And he turned to look coldly at Munsel.

Mills leaned forward, facing Lemke. He spoke very quietly.

'Herr Lemke, I am in a hurry. I have other things to do. I assure you that your operation is finished. Phone the apartment at Rathausstrasse if you wish. There will be no answer. I am prepared to trade with you if it doesn't take too long.'

'What do you mean? Trade.'

'I will trade your life for the details of who is running this operation at Moscow Centre.'

The muscles at the side of Lemke's mouth were knotted, but there were no other signs of fear apart from the anger in his voice as he spoke to Munsel.

'And you are party to this, Munsel?'

Mills cut in sharply. 'Cut out the moralizing, Lemke. Which do you want to do?'

Lemke stood up slowly and Mills stood up too. The Walther was out of his pocket, pointing at Lemke.

'You said I could phone the apartment.'

'I'll dial—you call the digits.'

They walked over to a long side-board and Mills picked up the phone.

'What's the code for Hamburg?'

'Oh—two—one.'

Mills dialled and then carried on as Lemke gave the numbers. He held the receiver to his ear and listened. You could feel the emptiness at the other end. That sad, lonely silence that quarrelling lovers and creditors know so painfully well. After a few moments he handed the receiver to Lemke who put it slowly to his ear. He stood there listening. He took almost three minutes before he put the phone back on its cradle. He stood with both hands resting on the sideboard, his head bowed in thought. Then he sighed and turned to Mills.

'What is it you want to know?'

'Who is directing the operation for the KGB in Hamburg.'

'Kirov. Sergei Kirov.'

'What's his address?'

'He is the Naval attaché in Bonn, at the Soviet Embassy.'

'His address in Hamburg.'

'He has no address here. He seldom comes here.'

'And who controls it in Moscow?'

'Ustenko—Eduard Ustenko.'

'Which directorate?'

'Second chief directorate.'

'Department?'

'A combined operation between third and fourth.'

'When was it due to start?'

'Later today.'

'Who were you to report to afterwards?'

'I was to meet Ustenko.'

'Where?'

'Wittenburg.'

Mills looked puzzled and Munsel chipped in.

'It's over the border, East Germany. There's a checkpoint about fifteen kilometres from here.'

Mills waved Lemke back to his chair. Lemke's strength and assurance had gone.

'Who else was involved apart from the people at the apartment?'

'Tiebert, nobody else.'

'When were you recruited?'

'When I did my officer training in Russia in 1934.'

'And you've worked for them ever since?'

'Yes.'

'Where's your radio and code pads?'

Lemke hesitated.

'What about my wife? D'you intend any action against her?'

'I assume that means your gear is at your home in Hamburg.'

Lemke nodded.

'Where was the meeting place in Wittenburg?'

Lemke shook his head.

'I won't discuss that.'

Mills turned to Munsel and handed him the pistol.

'I'm going to look around, Otto.'

Mills searched the house carefully but there was very little except a Russian passport with Lemke's photograph. It had been stuck with adhesive tape to the underside of one of the drawers in a small chest of drawers. There were two cases already packed with clothes.

Back downstairs Mills took over the pistol from Munsel.

'Where is your wife at the moment, Herr Lemke?'

'She's at our Hamburg house.'

'You're planning to stay on the other side, with the Russians. Why?'

'It was a precaution because of Tiebert's death.'

'How did you find out he was dead?'

'I phoned and the police answered. I got somebody to check at Police Headquarters. He thought they were suspicious that equipment had been removed. There will be an inquiry. I was advised to go to the other side and wait to see what happened.'

A bell rang for Mills and he hesitated, but he couldn't identify what it was about. He sensed a danger, something to notice that he hadn't noticed.

Just stay there, Lemke, don't move at all.' And Mills nodded for Munsel to join him. He partly closed the door and they stood in the hall.

'Otto. You go back to the car.'

'Why, David? What's the matter?'

Mills sighed and looked at Munsel's grim face.

'I've got to do it, Otto. I can't leave him running around. I've got to finish him.'

'In cold blood? After he's co-operated? After you implied that he'd be safe if he talked?'

'Otto, he's a traitor. Has been since 1934.'

'When Germany was down after World War I we were allowed no armed forces. The Russians were the only ones who helped. The only ones who trained our potential officers and pilots. Those men were bound to feel grateful to the Soviets.'

Mills shook his head.

'It won't wash, Otto. He's a danger. He could do it again.'

'They won't trust him after this debacle.'

'They'll have to trust him. He's too good for them not to use him. They'll use him some way.'

'Expose him then, but let him live. I'll stay. I'll hold him till you contact me. When you're on your way I'll call the police and hand him over.'

'That'll mean trouble for you, Otto. All sorts of questions. They may not even believe you. Remember, when they pass the word back to higher authority, higher authority won't want to know.'

'If they let him go the responsibility is theirs.'

'But why risk yourself, your reputation and all that?'

'The killing has to stop somewhere, David. Let it stop here.'

Mills tapped the barrel of the pistol against the palm of his hand. Then suddenly, impulsively, he gave the gun to Munsel.

'OK Otto. I've got his passport. I'll leave him with you. But I'll send one of my boys in to stay with you.' He looked across at Munsel and touched his arm. 'It's not what I planned but maybe you're right. Contact me in London through the Embassy.'

'Fine. Give Jutta my love.'

'Don't worry. I will.'

Mills had given instructions to the team and one of them went off to join Munsel. And now Mills sat with maps spread out on the back seat of the Volkswagen, planning his route to Büsum. There was no way to avoid crossing the city of Hamburg and even in the early hours of the morning there would be traffic enough to slow him down. He would need to average 40 m.p.h. over roads he barely knew. He slid the maps into the talc flaps and marked the route with the chinagraph pencil and tucked it back in its pocket.

He had been gone six minutes when the black Mercedes rolled to a stop just past the shops. A man cursed in the darkness as he stumbled on a stone but from then on they were silent. And when the watcher in the Volkswagen died, that too was sudden and silent. Just the strangled grunt as the hard hand went round his mouth and then the gush of air and gas as the knife came out of his chest.

Chapter 21

It had taken Mills fifteen minutes to reach the small airfield at Boburg, and as the winking lights on the control faded on his left, he headed for Hamburg. From the flyover where he crossed the E4 autobahn he took ten minutes to Ost-Weststrasse. And there he was held by the traffic lights at the History Museum. There was a police car parked alongside the St Pauli football ground at Heiligengeistfeld and he watched in the mirror but they made no move to follow. There were early-risers as he passed the Eidelstedt camping-site, as the road swung in a wide curve towards Pinneberg. Over to the right were the lights of the airport and three giant jets winked their lights as they lined up for take-off. At Elmshorn he stopped for petrol, and a sleepy night-porter at the Hamburgerhof came shivering out on to the front steps to point the way to a garage.

By Itzehoe there were lorries loaded down with vegetables and fruit for the market and at Heide the clock on the town-hall was striking six. There were ten more miles to go.

He drove right down to the edge of the beach at Büsum and in the distance he could see the morning sun glinting on the yellow fuselage of the helicopter. It was a Sikorski S61A and the rotors were already turning slowly and unevenly as he ran towards it. The tide was ebbing and the sand was still soft and wet. His legs ached as they carried his tired body to the man who stood on the sand, waiting. It was Rochford, his shirt ballooning out in the wind and his tie fluttering over his shoulder. He was waving his arms signalling to Mills to slow down.

For the last hundred yards all the accumulated exhaustion of the past few days seemed to concentrate in Mills' legs. There was a red haze behind his eyes and his breath seemed to burn in his lungs. He stumbled against Rochford who turned him to the steps. He held the steel frame but he couldn't move. A hand came down from the cabin, hauled him up, and pushed him into the nearest seat. He was aware of the girl's white face and Rochford's grim mouth as the door of the cabin was swung to. It had barely closed when the noise of the rotors clattered through his head, and as the helicopter lifted Mills closed his eyes.

It was almost three hours later when he came to, and the helicopter was swinging over a racetrack. The white rails, the grandstand and the ring of trees tilted as the pilot turned. They came down in a clearing in a small stand of silver birches and conifers, and the tall grass lay flat under the slip-stream from the rotors.

The pilot was talking softly into his radio, then he leaned forward and cut out the turbos, and there was a solid silence that made the sound of his heart seem like a giant pump in his ears. He twisted in his seat and looked across at Rochford and the girl. She smiled a faint smile as he stood up. The door swung open and McHugh was standing below with a man in a blue lounge suit.

As Mills waited for the girl he touched his face, it was burning hot and the stubble of his beard was thick and coarse. He held her hand as McHugh helped her down the metal ladder. Rochford waved to him to go first. McHugh took his arm and moved him clear of the helicopter. Mills saw a white building, with big square windows.

'Where the hell are we, Jim?'

'The other side of the trees it's Newcastle Race Course and the building over there's the hotel. We've booked rooms for you all for tonight. We can work out what happens after that when you've all had some rest.'

'You're up to date with the operation?'

'Yes. The surveillance team have signed off now. We've sent them down to Madrid. They'll be back in a couple of days. How up to date are you?'

'I haven't seen the reports from the stay-behind team but I'll check those later.'

McHugh nodded. 'Yes. All in good time. You get some sleep first.'

The girl was walking with the other man just ahead of them.

'Who's that fellow?'

'He's Pallant. He's a doctor.'

'What's he here for, for God's sake?'

'Going to give you a check-over and help the girl.'

Mills stopped and looked at McHugh.

'What makes you think she needs a doctor?'

McHugh put his hand on Mills' arm.

'David, I'm afraid Munsel's dead. We'll have to tell her.'

'Dead? What in hell happened?'

'We couldn't get a link from the team watching the apartments to the team you left at Lemke's house. So we sent the other team down to check. Both our chaps had been killed and so had Munsel and Lemke.'

'How?'

'Our two had been knifed. Lemke and Munsel were shot.'

'Those bastards. Those cunning bastards. And I should have known. They must have driven off and then circled back. I remember he said he'd been advised to go across the border. I never asked who advised him. What about his wife? She's in Lisbon, has anybody told her?'

'Our Embassy's checking. They haven't traced her yet. We're having to go very carefully because we assume the German Embassy will contact her. There's been no public announcement as yet but we know that they know. There's a hell of a row going on behind the scenes but the press don't seem to know. They'd rumble something if we chase after Frau Munsel when we're not supposed to know yet.

The Embassy's doing it's stuff so don't worry on that score.'

Mills clenched his fists in frustration. 'My God, what a shambles. What a mess, what a waste. Just when everything was coming right for Munsel and Jutta. You're sure, Jim? You're sure he's dead?'

'I'm sure, David.'

They walked in silence to the big glass entrance door and McHugh walked across for the keys to the rooms. When he came back to Mills he handed over two keys. 'If you need me, or Pallant, phone me in room 407. I'll keep Rochford down here for a bit.'

The lift was quick and smooth, and the girl leaned against the mirror and smiled up at him. He felt such sadness for her. Such sadness for them all. But he said,

'Well we made it, sweetie.'

Her arms went round his neck and the soft body clung to him.

Their rooms adjoined and between them was a large sitting-room whose windows looked out across the garden, the big car-park, and to the distant trees that lined the race course. As they looked out they heard the clacking of the helicopter as it rose from behind the trees, and then it was lost in the flare of the sun.

'Sweetie, why don't you sit down and I'll order some coffee and something to eat?'

'Tell me, David.'

'Tell you what?'

'Whatever it is. Something's the matter. Tell me quickly. Is it us?'

He shook his head and looked at the apprehensive face.

'It's your father. I'm afraid he's dead.'

The dry lips peeled apart.

'What happened?'

'He was shot.'

'Who shot him and why?'

He took both her hands and shook his head slowly. 'It's

best you don't know, love. I'll tell you some day, but not now.'

'Does mamma know?'

'I'm not sure. I think by now your embassy in Lisbon will have told her.'

She sat on the edge of the bed her fingers plucking the softness of the cover. Then she looked up at him and he was terribly aware of her attraction for him, the lovely face, the erotic body and the eagerness to please.

'What are we going to do, David. About us?'

'We could be married in three days.'

She half smiled. 'You still want to?'

'I do.'

'Then let's do that.'

He had walked down to McHugh's room. He was on the telephone and he waved Mills to one of the chairs where he sat down waiting for the phone call to finish. As McHugh replaced the receiver and turned to face Mills he saw the tiredness and tension on his face.

'How did it go, David?'

'Hard to tell. No tears, no fuss, but I guess they will come when it finally sinks in.'

'Anything we can do to help? What about getting her mother over? Would that help?'

Mills shook his head. 'Right now there's only one thing that will give her some security, and you could help with that.'

McHugh shrugged and smiled, 'Just say the word.'

'Can you fix us a special licence, a marriage licence, so that we can be married in the next few days?'

There was only a moment's hesitation, and then McHugh had said, 'Just leave it to me David. I'll get back to them now and see what the Judge Advocate's boys can do.' He stood up, 'Take it for granted that it will be done. Can I come up later and have a celebratory drink with you both?'

'She'd like that.'

* * *

They were married on a Friday morning in the Register Office in the Kings Road. Rochford had been best man. Mills had been paid off. Generously but not lavishly, and they had found a flat in Hampstead.

Mills started his own small advertising company and it prospered. There were times when he didn't sleep too well, and the moonlight across the heath became familiar.

It was nearly three years later when he came home one evening to meet that special silence that says nobody's there, and they're never going to be there again.

There was an envelope on the hall table. He picked it up and walked into their bedroom. He piled up the pillows and then ripped open the envelope. It was very short.

Dearest, dearest, David,

I love you so much. I always will. But I couldn't bear to let you down. I've gone away and I shall not come back.

I'll leave you in peace.

Your loving, loving, wife—
Jutta.

There were all her clothes in the wardrobe, their travel cases were still there, plastered with labels. Perfumes and cosmetics still lay in the drawer of her dressing table. It had been almost three months later when he noticed the brown paper parcel under the pile of shoes in the wardrobe. It was another diary. But this time the names were familiar, and the bundle of photographs showed that he had few friends. He'd known of course, without knowing. He had programmed his mind to reject the facts that wouldn't fit, the times that didn't add up, the phone conversations that were stilted with guilt, the familiar cars that left as he arrived, and all the mental barbed wire of deception. Many people can love those deserving of love, some play the saint and love the undeserving. And there's a price to pay for all such self-deception.

The heaped blue and green capsules in Mills' hand had looked iridescent and beautiful, they held their promise of peace and oblivion like jewels or precious stones. They went in his open mouth, clicking against his teeth, their smoothness melting on his tongue before the whisky washed them down. A patch of golden sunlight shimmered on the ceiling and as his head lay back on the pillows that was the last thing he saw. The papers said it was the hottest autumn day since records were kept.